The Lost Angel

Also by
ELIZABETH GOUDGE

The Lost Angel

stories

by

ELIZABETH GOUDGE

Decorations by Shirley Hughes

HODDER AND STOUGHTON
LONDON · SYDNEY · AUCKLAND · TORONTO

Contents

The Two Caves

The Two Caves

THERE was once a moment in time that defeated time. It was the moment when something pierced through the dark flood of the years as a crocus spear thrusts through the winter earth, to grow to a flower-like flame, die and live once more, never to die again.

It was the perfection of selfless love, the only eternal thing eternity itself, God. It burns at the heart of the world, in the heart of every living thing, in all wisdom, beauty, joy, pain and death.

The moment in history when it thrust up like this was when a man was born who would carry this perfection in his human body as a lantern carries the gold. Saint Augustus says of this moment that "God looked at us through the lattice of our flesh and he spake us fair."

It might have been thought that when this love thrust through the whole world would have known it. But actually hardly anyone knew, so quiet and humble a thing is love, our God.

The night of the coming was the night when poor people lit a lantern in their stable. They had not done that before, since the tired beasts did not need a light to go to sleep by, and they did not do it again, but that night they had to because a girl gave birth to her baby there. The inn was full and there was no other shelter.

The stable was only a cave in the rocky hillside but it held privacy and human kindness for the girl and her worried husband, and about midnight a son was born. He cried a little, but when he was put in his mother's arms he was happy and did not cry again.

And after that there was a deep silence in the little town until very early in the morning, while it was yet dark, some poor men came running; and they ran fast in eagerness because of some news that had been told them. For a moment they halted in the light that shone through the broken wood of the stable door, too awed to go in, and the beam from a star overhead silvered the hair and the beard of the oldest of them.

And then they bent their heads and entered the cave. They were there for a short while and when they came out there was a brightness in the eastern sky and the youngest said, "This cave is the heart of the world."

The child grew to be a man of great strength and vaster love and there was no experience known to men, joyous or appalling, peaceful or agonising, through which he did not in some way pass, leaving the gold of his love at the heart of it to shine upon us as each in our turn we come to the happy or hard things of our life.

But the eyes of perfect love were too piercing to be met easily by evil men, and though he spake them fair in love and compassion he also spake them straight and hard in truth and anger, and so they killed him under the hot sun, and at evening buried his body in a cave in the hillside.

But very early in the morning, while it was yet dark, the feet of poor men came running; and they ran fast in eagerness because of some news that had been told them. When they came to the cave they halted for a moment in awe, because the stone that had closed it had been rolled away, and the light from the morning star silvered the head and the beard of the oldest of them. Then they bent their heads and went into the cave.

After a while they came out, and the east was turning to gold. The young man said, "He is risen." The older one said nothing, for with grief and joy he was past the power of audible speech, but in his heart he said, "An empty tomb is now at the heart of the world."

And so there were these two caves that were really the same cave, because each was at the heart of the world, and these two great happenings, a birth and a re-birth that were the same birth. And because love lives forever in the heart, all shall be well.

The Silver Horse

The Silver Horse

I

THOUGH SHE HAD scarcely slept all night Delia was wide awake with the first gleam of day. The sun saw to that, flooding the window with light, gently touching her. He's kind today, she thought. He could be angry, blood-red behind the headland of Mynydd Melin across the estuary, or sullen and lowering, sulphur-yellow with the spleen of thunder. But this milk-white and silver gentleness boded no harm and she pushed the window wide open. Sitting up she leaned her elbows on the sill, her chin in her hands. The air, cool from the sea and from the night, did not come in this morning upon wings, for there was no wind, but lapped in over the sill as gently as the ripples upon the crescent of gleaming sand beyond the river. Though the sky was already luminous, wreaths of mist hung over the river and Mynydd Melin rose up out of a billowing whiteness that hid the rocks and the caves along the shore, but did not hide the ruined house of Henllys, or the white road that wound up towards the mountain, Carn-Inglis. These two, the house and the mountain, both had such starkness in the morning light that Delia flinched. Or perhaps the starkness was only something that she imagined because this morning she hated them both; even Carn-Inglis to whose great presence she had looked up morning by morning all her life and until now had thought of as her friend. But now he was no longer a friendly mountain but the entrance to the abomination of desolation. The road, that led into the great world round the flanks of Carn-Inglis, passed through a chasm in the rocks shaped like a gateway. Delia gazed at this as once Adam gazed at the gate of the Garden of Eden through which he must pass for ever; because of what he had done.

"And I have done it," Delia whispered to herself. "It's I who decided we must go. Oh God, I was mad!"

Despair made her feel sick and cold, and wrenching her gaze away from the gateway she looked instead at the house of Henllys, and then she was hot with anger, suddenly strong and invigorated with it. For the young squire lived there all by himself in that ruined gloomy old house. Or to be more accurate he lived there occasionally, so occasionally that she had never even seen him. But you can hate people without seeing them if they have been unkind to you, and the squire was turning her and the children out of the cottage because they could not pay the rent. She had written to him herself, a letter that had taken her hours of hard labour to write because she was a scholar neither by nature nor training, begging him to give her time, but his bailiff had answered the letter because the squire was away and he had said she and the children must go. They were going today.

She had been sorry for the young squire once, sorry that the old squire, his uncle, should have left him such a ruined and desolate inheritance. And she had been sorry for him all over again when his adored horse had been stolen; though people said it served him right for teaching it to stop at every pub. He was just such another as his uncle. But now she wasn't sorry any more because you can't be sorry for people who turn you out of your home.

It was not the cottage itself that Delia minded leaving, it was the place. They had lived in several cottages during the sixteen years of her life and this one was damp and its shadows at night were haunted by her mother's death. It was the place. She knew no other. The world where they were going, the tumultuous world beyond the gateway, held for her this morning only the terror of the unknown. And it was she who had decided they must go there. And now it was too late to change her mind.

She wept a few heartbroken tears, her fists stuck in her eyes, and then rubbed them dry to look her last upon her Eden. The tide was going out and the boats in the harbour lay sprawling on the sand, the little river threading its way beside them to the sea. Delia looked for the herons. They were sometimes here in the early morning when the mists still lay over the river and before the harbour had woken to life. They were shy birds and with the first banging door, the first echo of a voice, they would be gone. Leaning far out of the small window she looked for them and found them, first one and then another. They stood upright by the river on the far side, delicate dream-shapes half hidden and half revealed by the mist. They stood as though charmed into stillness, meditative, creatures of another world as well as of this one. Delia had always been aware of the herons' world but she did not know what it was. Certain creatures, certain sounds and scenes, belonged to it, and in dreams she fancied she sometimes breathed its air, but it had no tangible reality.

It was midsummer day, eighteen ninety-one, holding the promise of a fair day and yet the day of doom. Delia looked back over her shoulder at the little room with its whitewashed walls and trodden earth floor, and the truckle-beds of the children set one on each side of the space where once the carved chest had stood. But not now. Their treasures had gone. She had gradually sold them to the old man who kept The Shop in Trawscoed, a little town four miles away, through the lane and over the hill behind the cottage. She had sold them to help pay the rent. They had gone one by one, first the chest her father had made, then the patchwork quilt and the lustre jugs. Each departure had been like the drawing of a tooth but it had been worth while to stay here. It had been when there were no more treasures that she had no longer been able to pay the rent.

On the floor, where the chest had stood, there was now a neat bundle, their clothes fastened up in a cotton check tablecloth. Leaning against the bundle was a large green umbrella and in front of it a row of four pairs of boots, patched and shabby but carrying a high and gallant polish. A pile of freshly laundered garments lay on top of a stool, crowned by a black straw bonnet, and the sight of these things crushed Delia's heart with a terrible sense of immediacy. In an hour's time the carrier's cart would be here. In three hours' time they would be in a train, a thing they had never even seen. By the end of the day they would be in the unknown city where lived their father's brother and his childless wife with the needle-sharp eyes. They would live with them in the city, in the house beside the railway track of which their mother had told them, where the curtains were always grimy however often you washed them. She would go to work at the mill, and so would the other children as soon as they were old enough, and people said it was very kind of their uncle and his wife to take pity on their orphan nephews and nieces; four of them, Delia, Dewi, Megan and Tom.

Was it possible, Delia thought suddenly, that their uncle's wife, reputed to be not very strong, waking perhaps at this moment to the rattle of the trains beyond the grimy window pane, also felt that this midsummer day was the day of doom? This was an aspect of the affair that had not hitherto occurred to her. But now she remembered her uncle's wife upon the one occasion when she had visited them, and how apprehensive she had seemed when the twins Megan and Tom, then two years old, had come too near with their noise and laughter. The twins were five now but just as noisy, and Dewi, aged nine, had a fiery temper. Poor Aunt Eliza! Delia, divided from the others by the deaths of two intermediate children, had since her father's loss at sea always felt nearer in age to her mother than to the younger children, and could understand the adult point of view. As she quickly dressed herself in her clean clothes, and went into the kitchen to start the children's breakfast, she felt very sorry indeed for Aunt Eliza, and for Uncle Reuben too, who would no doubt suffer from the backwash of his wife's distress.

Why had their mother had to die like that, just of a chill on the chest that had turned into pneumonia? While her mother lived they had managed so well, taking in Mrs. Griffiths's washing and cleaning at the Rectory. But alone she had not managed so well. Mrs. Griffiths had grumbled about her ironing and sent the washing elsewhere, and the Rector's new wife had said she left cobwebs in the corners. When she had first got into real difficulties neighbours had helped her, but their patience had finally given out and the Rector had written to her uncle. He had done his duty. He'd offered them all a home and she

had accepted his offer. But she knew now that she had made a
mistake. Yet what else could I have done? she demanded of fate
as she uncovered the ashes, laid driftwood on them, and then
when the flames leapt up set upon the fire the old black saucepan
with the children's porridge in it. It was goodbye to the old black
saucepan. Their beds, a few bits of furniture and their pots and
pans had been sold already to a neighbour to pay the last of their
debts. He would fetch them away when she had gone. She had
nothing now but the railway tickets that her uncle had sent her,
hung round her neck in a little bag, but she was solvent. Her
mother would have been pleased about that. But not about anything else. She had loved this place as passionately as Delia
herself. "Don't leave it, Delia," she had said once.

What else could I have done? There was no answer and she woke
the children, dressed and fed them, and answered the twins' eager
questions about the train and the big city as well as she could.
Dewi said nothing, merely scowled and ate. Come what might he
could always eat; he ate, his mother had been wont to say, like a
cormorant, disdaining mastication. But it was not like him to
scowl and she wondered what he was thinking. Ever since he had
first set eyes on a horse he had wanted to be a groom. Was he
thinking of the mill where he would work and the absence of
horses there? His bowl of porridge finished, and polished round
with a crust of bread, he looked up from under the thatch of
wild black hair that shadowed his forehead and gave her a glance
of sheer hatred out of wide-open clear grey eyes. At first, coming
from such an affectionate boy, the hatred gave her a profound
shock, and then in the midst of her wretchedness she had a
sudden feeling of elation, as though their spirits had struck
together like flint and tinder. She said nothing to justify herself,
merely held his eyes with her own as she handed over her own
untouched bowl of porridge. He ate it practically at the one
intake, polished the bowl once more and ate the crust. Though
nothing in their situation was apparently changed she went
about the final tasks with light in her mind, not much light but
a faint glimmering like a candle flame in a dark room.

2

ONE KNEW WHEN Owen the Cart was coming because of the barking of the outriders, the two black and white mongrel dogs who always accompanied him. Looking out of the window, tying on her bonnet, Delia saw Harry the younger dog racing along beside the river barking at the gulls. The herons had gone now and the mists were lifting. Beyond the gulls, on an island of sand in the middle of the bay, the oyster catchers were still asleep. They had been piping all night and she had heard their familiar music in the intervals of her fitful sleep. Beyond them again stood three cormorants, wings outspread as though hung out to dry, and she smiled at their comicality as she always did. Even this morning she could not help smiling. Somewhere inland a cuckoo was calling and from near at hand there was a shout. Owen the Cart was waiting for them by the harbour wall. The cliff path in front of the cottage was too narrow for him to bring the cart to the door and they must carry their gear down. It was only a short way and she and Dewi carried the bundle easily between them. The dark, black-eyed twins followed behind. They were no longer chattering. Tom's eyes were round and solemn and Megan had her thumb in her mouth. They had suddenly realized what was happening.

From the front of the small hooded cart Owen eyed them with kindness. He did not get down to help them because he was old and bow-legged. His white hair and beard stirred in the little wind that was now blowing down the world. The horse between the shafts did not turn its head but Bob, the old dog, came towards them with slowly wagging tail. Delia bent to caress him so as not to have to meet Owen's eyes. She was aware of the cottages standing round the harbour, whitewashed or coloured blue or ochre, with fuchsias in their small front gardens and geraniums in their windows. Behind the geraniums, she knew, eyes were watching, but she did not look at the windows. She had said her goodbyes already. She got quickly into the cart, pulling the twins up after her, and Dewi handed up the bundle and followed with his under lip stuck out. She sat on the bundle, the twins standing at her knee, and Dewi sat on the footboard with his legs swinging. Owen the Cart

swore at the horse, Harry and Bob barked loudly and the caval-
cade moved off across the harbour, in and out between the
bright hulls of the boats, splashed through the little river and
went on over the sand towards the road that wound up over
Mynydd Melin. They had never yet travelled far upon this
road, only up to the top of the headland where the wind blew
keenly over the heather and bracken . . . Though once Delia and
Dewi had left the road and walked to the Lion Rock above the
Bay of the Seals, where the waves moved in the great caves, and
where in the spring the white seal calves lay on the beach of
coloured stones basking in the sun. They had lain on the rock
and watched the seals but they had not dared to go down and
creep close. Delia had told herself that the seals, like the herons,
were denizens of two worlds . . . They had never gone anywhere
near the dreaded gateway in the rocks of Carn-Inglis for it had
always frightened them.

Usually it seemed a long way across the bay but now it was
as though the wind was behind them. Noah, Owen the Cart's
old grey horse, was usually a slow mover but today he pulled
the cart lurching over the sand at a fine pace, and then whirled
up the dusty white road between the drystone walls as though
its weight were a mere nothing to him.

"Whatever has happened to Noah?" gasped Delia.

"It's not Noah," said Owen the Cart.

"No," said Dewi in a whisper of tense excitement. It was
impossible for him to be too miserable to notice equine details
and with his first glance he had known that this horse was not
Noah. "Where is Noah?" he asked.

"The knacker's yard," said Owen the Cart gloomily.

Delia gave a cry of distress, for Noah was an old friend, and
the tears she had been fiercely holding back suddenly overflowed
and ran down her cheeks. She wept silently. Megan, taking her
thumb out of her mouth, roared her grief. Tom was unmoved
and Dewi merely demanded, "Owen, where did you get that
horse?"

"Bought him in Pontmeddyg Market," said Owen.

"That's a lie," said Dewi. He knew about horses as well as
loved them. Owen, who had lived alone in his whitewashed cabin
in a state of outward poverty for as long as anyone could remember, was reputed to be wealthy, with bags of money stored

up the chimney, but he was also 'very near' and psychologically incapable of parting with enough silver to purchase this fleet young horse. And it was well known in the district that Owen the Cart did not buy things. He came by them.

"Got a face like a crocodile," said Owen. "In very poor condition."

Dewi, concentrated upon the horse, made no answer. As to the physiognomy he must, from his position in the rear, remain ignorant at present, but he noticed now, as the road rose more steeply and the pace slowed, that the poor beast was very thin, badly galled and with a staring unkept coat. Yet he was a glorious beast! He had a gallant heraldic head, with a full mane of silvery flowing hair. He had looked a queer sort of dull brown down below on the sands but now that they mounted up into the sunshine streaks of silver shone through the dun colour. And a willing cheerful beast. When the road became so steep that he could only toil upwards at a slow straining walk he strained with courage. Dewi leapt from the cart and went to walk beside his head, to lighten the load, and after a moment Delia did the same. One on each side of him they wished they could peer round the blinkers and see if he was really crocodile-faced, but a certain delicacy forbade them. It did not seem polite to do that. Instead they fell back a few paces and took hold of the shafts and pulled with a will. The horse rewarded them with fresh efforts and almost at a trot they came to the top of the hill.

But here he stopped for at the summit the Golden Lion, one of the oldest inns in the country, stood four square to the winds of the world. He stopped as though accustomed to stop but he did not let his heraldic head droop down in weariness. He held it high still, and the silver mane lifted in the keen wind. If he was tired he disdained to show it. It was Owen the Cart who lifted his battered old hat with a weary sigh and passed his forearm across his forehead, his blue eyes meanwhile rolling round to the inn door, wistful as the eyes of a saint gazing into heaven. He moistened his lips with the tip of his tongue, put his hand in his pocket and brought it out again trembling and empty. Dewi also put his hand in his pocket and to Delia's astonishment brought out the silver sixpence the Rector had given him for weeding the garden and cleaning out the stable, and which she thought he had spent on toffee months ago. He reached up and pressed it into Owen the Cart's trembling hand and in less time than it takes to tell Owen had vanished. After that it seemed to Delia that everything happened at once and passed almost instantly beyond her control. Dewi leapt up into the cart, pulling her after him, and standing upright like a Roman charioteer he seized the reins and shook them. "Go, boy, go!" he whispered to the dun and silver horse, and like the wind the horse went.

Delia clung to her seat in the perilously swaying cart and the twins clung to her. Harry the young dog was with them, racing at full stretch, but Bob the old dog had stayed behind. That, Delia thought, was just as well for their present speed was not suited to the elderly. Yet she was not frightened for she felt again that sudden feeling of elation that she had known when her spirit and Dewi's had struck together like flint and tinder. She realized now that in that wordless contact she had acknowledged her mistake and he had told her he would deliver them if he could. It was Dewi and the horse who were now striking sparks from each other and she trusted them and was glad she did, for she could no more have halted their fiery union than she could have halted a shooting star.

They seemed on the top of the world, up here on the summit of Mynydd Melin with the wind roaring in their ears. The flat fields with their drystone walls stretched on either side and in them the sheep were feeding, and the black and white cattle. Here and there a low farmhouse crouched to the ground, sheltering behind its thicket of bushes, all bent one way by the wind from the sea. Beyond the last western wall heather and bracken bordered the long blue line of the sea, a deep blue now that the sun was up in a clear sky, unbelievably blue like the wild hyacinths in the spring. Foxgloves grew in the ditches on either side of the road and harebells on the grass verges. To the east upon their right rose the mountain and even now the road was turning eastward towards it. That deadly gateway in the rocks was coming close, was almost upon them, and Carn-Inglis was suddenly full of a dark terror. Were they not escaping after all? Were they going through? Delia glanced anxiously at Dewi but he was perfectly serene, holding the reins firmly but making no attempt either to urge the horse on or to hold him back.

"But we are coming to the gate, Dewi," she said. "We're nearly there."

"Yes," said Dewi.

"But once we're through it we come to—you know."

"Yes."

"But we don't want to go where we're going."

"We want to go where he's going," said Dewi and he jerked his wild black head towards the horse.

"But where is he going?"

"Shut your mouth, Delia," said Dewi suddenly.

She was silent, for he was quite right. Only fools chattered and protested when fate was carrying them along to the rapids, sensible people were silent and held on; as the twins were doing, clutching her knees and swaying easily to the movements of the cart, bright-eyed and red-cheeked with excitement, a little afraid yet ready for anything. She began to understand something, a new bit of knowledge about being alive. If in a crisis you make the best decision you can, even the wrong one, and then lose control of the consequences through no fault of your own, don't worry. When you have done all you can fate takes control and is not blind.

3

THEY WERE AT the gate, whirling in through the dark portals, and then they were through, in a narrow rocky gorge and going slowly again because the road was steep. There was no sudden change such as Delia had been half expecting, no screaming of trains and clang of dark satanic mills, but because they were out of the wind here and going slowly, a sudden deep silence. It awed them so much that Delia and Dewi forgot to get out to lighten the load for the horse. Instead they sat where they were and listened to it and as always when one listens to silence they found it had a voice. And then a second voice and a third, or else the same voice with many notes, like a harp with many strings.

At first it was the voice of water, a hidden stream falling down the rocks, and then as they climbed higher and the walls of the gorge opened out to the bare flanks of the mountain it was larks singing, and mysteriously woven into the larks' song came the distant cry of curlews. And then came the distant tinkling of sheep bells and then once more the voice of the wind; not the roar in their ears that it had been but a soft humming as though the heather were already in flower with the bees stirring over it.

Dewi had dropped the reins altogether and so it was not his fault that the horse left the road for a rough cart track leading to the left. Not that he would have tried to prevent him had the reins still been in his hands, because the horse was in charge. But later on he found it convenient to tell an irate yet relieved Uncle Reuben, and an infuriated Owen the Cart, that it had not been his fault.

"We've left the road," said Delia.

"It's still a road," said Dewi.

"Not a proper one," said Megan.

"Not *the* road," said Tom.

"So we aren't going to the trains," said Megan.

"Then where are we going?" asked Tom.

"Who cares?" asked Dewi. "If we aren't going where we *were* going who cares where we *are* going?"

"When shall we have our dinner?" asked Megan, who like Dewi was fond of her food. "Delia, when shall we have our dinner?"

With horror Delia realized that the sandwiches she had cut had in the grief of departure been left behind. But Dewi answered for her. "At the house," he said.

"What house?" asked Tom.

"At the house where the horse lives."

"What's it like?" asked Megan, and Delia noticed with apprehension that her lower lip was trembling.

"There are apple trees and raspberries at the gate," she said hastily, saying anything that came into her head to prevent Megan roaring.

"And new bread in the larder?" asked Megan. "Yellow butter? Fried sausages, crunchy outside and soft and juicy inside?"

"Stop it, Megan!" said Dewi desperately. Food had been short in their home for months past and her recital was making his mouth water like a tap turned on, and his empty stomach flap up and down inside him like one of those flags of distress that shipwrecked mariners fly on rafts at sea. Only no one could see his flag of distress. He wished he could fly it from the top of his head. "If you don't stop it," he said, "I'll knock all your teeth out so you'll never crunch again."

He was crimson in the face and Delia was afraid he was going to fall into one of his rages. She couldn't stand his rages. Abruptly she felt that there wasn't much more she would be able to stand, not without a cup of tea. No doubt the heavenly harp music was still sounding, and she could see with half a glance that beauty was about them like the banners of a king's passing, but her powers of appreciation were not what they had been. She addressed the horse. "Do you never get tired and hungry and thirsty?" she asked him.

The moment she had spoken she was sorry, for looking at him she saw that his coat was dark with sweat and that for the first time in their acquaintance his head was hanging as he dragged them farther and farther away from the trains, the mill, the darkness and the dirt. Harry, too, who had accompanied them so faithfully all this way, was whacked, his tail drooping and his tongue hanging out as he panted his way upward. She was out of the cart in a flash and so were the others, she and the twins pulling at the shafts with a will and Dewi pushing behind. They all felt better now. They could smell the honeysuckle covering the stone walls that bordered the track and feel the wind like the stroking of cool hands on their hot cheeks.

Presently the track widened out into a grassy hollow under a group of trees, and from under a green bank a spring bubbled up. They all stopped and the children flung themselves to the ground in the grass beside it and drank, cupping their hands to lift the cool water, and it was better than any cup of tea. And then the horse and Harry drank, long and deeply, and the horse ate grass while the children and Harry lay and watched him with envy, for though the water had slaked their thirst it had not quenched their hunger.

"He *is* like a crocodile," whispered Delia, watching the horse.

"He's not!" said Dewi, with all the more indignation because secretly he knew she was right. It was because the mouth was so large and opened so wide. Yet the countenance was no less attractive because it fell short of perfection. The eyes were dark and lustrous, the muzzle soft as velvet. The beautiful ears were most delicately shaped and on the noble forehead shone a white star.

"Look how he holds himself!" whispered Dewi, infatuated.

"And the mouth being so big it's as though he smiled at us," said Delia. And indeed it did seem as though they were approved of, so kindly did the lustrous eyes shine upon them, and so gently did the horse lower his proud head for the twins to caress his star.

"He looks lighter than he was," Delia went on. "And more streaky."

"He's sweated so much that some of the dye has run down."

"Dye?"

"He's not really a streaky-brown horse," Dewi said. "I saw that at once. He's been dyed brown. He's a silver-grey horse. I'm calling him Silver."

"But why should anyone want to dye him?" asked Delia.

"They would if they'd stolen him. So he shouldn't be recognized. You don't see a horse like this every day."

Suddenly Silver threw up his head, neighed as though in greeting to some unseen friend, and moved forward. The children only just had time to bundle up into the cart before they were in motion again, bumping over the grassy tussocks of the dell.

The track led them under an arch of trees and then they were out in the open again at the top of a hill, looking down into a small valley. It lay in a hollow of the mountains that were cupped like a hand to hold it. There was a patchwork of coloured fields, a stream running under a little humped bridge and a whitewashed cottage shining out like a pearl from its setting of ochre-washed stable and barn and green orchard trees. It was all very clear and small and looked infinitely removed from them, like one of those scenes upon which the dreamer gazes in the last moment before waking, aware of the burden of living once more fastening on his limbs like manacles yet straining back after the vanishing beauty. It belonged, Delia thought suddenly, in the world of the herons, those birds who vanished at the first sound of a banging door.

"It's not real," she said. "We can't go there."

"Silly, we *are* going there," said Dewi.

It was true. The track went there. It curved steeply down through a green field where sheep were feeding, humped itself over the bridge and disappeared into the orchard trees towards the cottage, and Silver was slithering down the track between

banks covered with foxgloves and honeysuckle. Upon one side
the stream that had come from the spring above ran down
through a tunnel of green ferns, bound for the larger stream
below. It tinkled gaily over the stones and the scent of the
honeysuckle came in great warm gusts.

"Look, the sea!" cried Tom.

Through a break in the hills opposite they could see a triangle
of blue and another track that led up to it and disappeared
into it. To the right of the track, on the crest of the hill, was a
strange outcrop of rock shaped like a lion.

"The Lion Rock," said Dewi. "Down below is the Bay of the
Seals. From here it's no distance at all."

"There's a heron by the stream," said Megan.

He stood among yellow irises, and when the cart swayed over
the humped-back bridge quite close to him he did not fly away.
The patchwork fields were bright to see but very small, a couple
of shorn hayfields tawny in the sun, clover, mustard, and a bean-
field smelling even sweeter than the honeysuckle. They looked to
Dewi more like the fields of a man who is playing at being a
farmer rather than actually being one. Delia was incapable just
now of such down to earth thoughts, but she was never at any
time so practical as Dewi and it did not seem to her strange that
when they drove into the orchard between old stone gateposts
overgrown with raspberries, the gate being lost, they should find
the grass below the wind-twisted trees bright with tiger lilies
of the same golden ochre as the barn and stable behind the
cottage. But Dewi let out a low whistle, and then another when
he saw the lantern hanging from the yew tree that faced the
mounting block across the path leading to the cottage door.

Silver stopped.

"You go in," Dewi commanded Delia. "You and Megan and
Tom. Harry and I will take Silver round to the stable and rub
him down."

Delia did as he told her. She was incapable of doing anything
else. He handed down the bundle and she and Tom carried it
up the path, Megan following with the umbrella. The cottage,
stoutly built of whitewashed stone, had windows on either side
of the front door and two small dormer windows in the thatch
above. Upon each windowsill stood a large white shell. Hidden
behind the shell next to the door on the right was the key.

Delia found it before she knew she was looking for it, put it in
the keyhole, turned it and pushed the door open.

4

THE ROOM INSIDE had a flagstone floor and a bright rag rug
before the hearth, where the ashes lay dead. There was an oak
table in the centre of the room, a settle by the hearth and a
dresser where rows of shining lustre jugs hung from their hooks.
There were some touches of luxury; a copper kettle by the
hearth, a beautiful china teaset on the high mantelshelf, a shelf
full of books and cushions on the settle, but otherwise the room
had for Delia a sense of familiarity. But she did not like the cold
hearth. It was a part of her religion, as it had been of her mother's,
always to have the flame on the hearth, and she opened a cupboard door in the wall and found, as she had expected, wood
and dried heather and flint and tinder. In a moment she had the
flames dancing and the shadows leaping. Now the room was
alive. Pulling off her bonnet she sighed with satisfaction. She
was, she found, alone. The twins had found another cupboard
door, with steep stairs inside, and were upstairs exploring the
little attic rooms. She could hear their delighted voices overhead.
She was glad to be alone. She stood for a moment or two, as
though listening for footsteps, and then because the traveller
did not come yet she ceased to listen and began to explore this
known and yet unknown home. Behind the living room there
was a little scullery and through its tiny window she could see
the well beside the back door. Then she opened the door of the
room on the other side of the front door. Inside was the bedroom.
A chest stood against the wall and a patchwork quilt was on the
bed.

She stood for a long time staring at the quilt, staring harder
and harder because it was so like the one her great grandmother
had made, and that she had sold to The Shop. It had been harder
to part with that quilt than with any of the other treasures
because her mother had been so fond of it, and had told her the
history of almost every patch; how that blue delaine sprigged
with pink roses had been great grandmother's wedding dress, and

that black bombazine with white stars Great Aunt Hannah's Sunday best, and the striped red and green poplin great grandmother's best. It was not until she had identified those three patches and several others that Delia realized that it was the same quilt. Her head swam and she clutched the bed post for support, and then sat down suddenly on the bed. As the world steadied about her once more her hands explored the quilt, feeling again the familiar warmth of it, lined with the wool of the sheep her great grandfather had kept on The Mountain. He had been a prosperous sheep farmer, his wife according to family tradition a fine lady, and Delia's mother had been proud of good blood in her veins. Delia looked at the chest against the wall and it was the one her father had made from wood washed up from a wreck. He had carved two herons on the lid. She got up and went back to the living room, to the dresser, and found her mother's three best lustre jugs among the others hanging from the hooks. They seemed to gather to themselves all the light of the fading day. She turned round and saw that mist was coming in from the sea. Its cold breath made her realise that she was shivering and going to the cupboard she put more wood on the fire.

She was crouched in front of the flames, warming herself, when she heard the footsteps she had been listening for and rose unsteadily to her feet. Rapid and vigorous, they came up the path, and then halted while the returning traveller looked for the key behind the shell. Not finding it he swore and then flung the door open and strode in. He seemed to fill the little room, his red head almost touching the rafters and his boots loud on the stone flags, a large dumbfounded young man in a full-skirted tawny riding-coat with bulging pockets. For a moment, in the light of the leaping flames, Delia saw very clearly a pair of golden-brown eyes staring at her, a large mouth dropping open and a freckled face crimsoning with shock and astonishment. Then she swayed and fell into his arms, knowing as she fell what was the matter with her. Breakfast was hours and hours ago and she hadn't had any. From miles away she heard her voice saying very slowly and clearly, "I want a cup of tea." Then everything went black.

When she came round again she was lying on the settle, the kettle was singing on the fire and the twins were sitting on the floor eating sugar buns. The large young man was standing up, emptying his bulging pockets of their packages. He brought out a string of sausages, unwrapped, a piece of cold pork inadequately wrapped, part of a loaf of bread, a hunk of cheese, a packet of sugar, a pat of butter folded in a cabbage leaf, and dropped them on the floor beside the bag of buns which already lay there dangerously near to his earthy booted feet. He grinned encouragingly at Delia and said, "Have a bun." Delia shook her head and said irritably, "I want a cup of tea. Did you buy them?"

"What?"

"My mother's things."

He shook his head in mystification, the kettle boiled and he took the teapot from the mantelpiece and made the tea. The door opened and Dewi came in with Harry at his heels. "Another of you?" ejaculated the large young man, and ran a hand rather wildly through his untidy red hair. "And a dog. You'd better pull the table up. Where have you just come from?"

"The stable," said Dewi, pulling up the table. "I've been rubbing my horse down."

"The devil you have," said the large young man. "So you've got a horse, have you? That's more than I have at the moment." Absentmindedly he poured out a cup of strong black tea, put four lumps of sugar in it, but no milk as there wasn't any, and handed it to Delia. "Pony or cob?"

Dewi's head went up. "A silver stallion," he said with infinite pride and scorn.

The young man's head also went up, or rather jerked up, the light of the fire entangled in his red hair as though it flamed in sudden outrage. "The devil," he said softly. "A silver stallion?" Then suddenly their eyes met and locked with intense sympathy, the sympathy of two men who have the same consuming passion, and in a moment or two they were deep in talk while saucers, plates, knives and forks, dealt out by the young man's flexible wrist, flew into place on the table like a pack of cards. The talk, the flying crockery, had purpose; they dismissed the suspicion that had formed above an aching chasm of grief and loss. It was this underlying purpose of generosity of which Delia was first aware when, made new by the hot sweet tea, she sat up on the settle. It showed in the man's mouth and eyes and his headlong movements, yet she also recognized it as something she already knew about. From the mystery of this she passed to a recognition of his state of hunger. Catching a flying saucer in her hands she said, "If you've a frying pan and some fat, I'll fry the sausages."

"Under the settle. Lard in the cupboard," said the young man, and went on talking about horses. Delia took the frying pan from under the settle, emptied out two spiders, picked up the sausages from the floor and set to work. In ten minutes' time they were all seated round the table, with Harry before the fire with his plateful, eating and talking with the pleasure of an affectionate family reunited after a long parting. Now and then, over the twins' dark heads, the young man looked at Delia and smiled, and she smiled back, in mutual amusement at something one of the children had said. For some time he appeared to take his peculiar situation entirely for granted, asking no questions, but after a while, as the children's chatter put him in possession of the facts, he began to ask a few, but quietly, slipping them in too gently to cause alarm, even though the questions themselves were not without a keen edge.

"So this horse is not really yours but Owen the Cart's?" he said to Dewi, his eyes very bright and keen. "In fact you've stolen him?"

Dewi flushed but met the straight look straightly. "No, it wasn't stealing. It was just that I recognized him and we went away together."

"Recognized him?"

"I'd been saving up for him. I knew when I saw him he was mine. I'd saved two shillings but sixpence went to Owen the Cart, for a drink, to get him out of the way."

"So that *you* could get out of the way?"

"Yes. So that we could go somewhere else, not to the mills, I don't want to work in a mill. I want to be a groom."

"And you thought the horse would bring you to where you could be a groom?"

"Well, I knew he'd bring me to where I could groom *him*."

"I still think you stole that horse," said the young man.

"No," said Dewi obstinately. "Owen the Cart stole him. Owen said he bought him at Pontmeddyg Market but Owen would never buy a horse. Owen doesn't buy things. He comes by them. So I didn't steal the horse. When you take what's been stolen already that's not stealing."

"Why not?"

Dewi gave a great sigh of despair. It appeared that he and the young man had an entirely different code of morals, and that can create a difficult situation between two otherwise sympathetic people. How he hated morals! Why couldn't they let them alone and concentrate on horses? The young man seemed to think so too for the food being now all eaten he pushed his chair back and said, "Come on out to the stable and show me the beast . . . Look there! Look at the weather!"

The sea mist was muffled so closely against the window that nothing could be seen at all. The orchard and the tiger lilies, the valley with its patchwork fields, the hills and the sea had all gone. Even the lantern and the yew tree had vanished. Delia told herself that they had disappeared as the herons had disappeared this morning. They were the other world and now the curtain was drawn. She wondered if she would ever see them again.

"Looks to me as though you'll all have to spend the night," said the young man with dismay.

Dewi and the twins looked at him in profound astonishment. Well, of course they were going to spend the night. They'd come to stay. Didn't he know that? It seemed he didn't for he turned questioningly to Delia and for the first time, so it seemed to him, looked at her. He was not in the habit of looking at women for throughout his life he had disliked them. From an indifferent stepmother and the heavy-handed nursemaids of his childhood, on through strident barmaids, large dowagers and giggling girls peeping from behind fans, he had hated them all. Friends and relations kept telling him he must marry and settle down, stop sowing wild oats and become respectable. But respectability scared him. He could entertain the idea of becoming eccentric or mad or wicked or even, astonishing thought, good, but not respectable. The thought of sitting beside the fire in a stuffy curtained room, wax fruit under a glass case on the mantelpiece, watching one of the giggling girls growing old and fat gave him claustrophobia.

This girl would never grow fat. She was fine drawn yet with a supple strength in her slenderness. Her hair, smooth and shining, plaited and twisted round her small head in a coronet, was nut brown. The bones of her face showed too clearly through the skin but they were good bones and her mouth was sweet and firm. The children were nice little brats but they had not got her quality; something brought there perhaps from afar, like sunlight in the water of a stream. Yet she was a working woman in the sense of a woman to whom work is second nature, and the dignity and zest of life. Her hands, broad, strong and scarred, showed that, and her air of maturity. Looking at her he was conscious of a feeling for her that he had never yet felt for a woman, respect. Yet she was touchingly young, too young for him to be calling her a woman. It was because the word girl had such claustrophobic connotations in his mind . . . The woman . . . For how long had he been standing here staring at her whilst she looked back at him, her grey eyes direct and unflinching, without either coquetry or embarrassment, simply wondering with him what they ought to do?

Suddenly he knew. "You and the little girl must have my room," he said. "I'll sleep upstairs with the boys."

"Is there a mattress upstairs?" she asked.

"No, but it doesn't matter. We'll get some hay from the stable and bed down on the floor. What we do tomorrow we'll decide tomorrow. All I know tonight is that you four can't go to the city and work in the mills."

He had taken charge, Delia realized, taking on from Silver. He looked very large and strong in the firelight, his hair very bright above his tanned face. He and the horse were silver and gold, moon and sun. In her weary brain they seemed to merge together.

"Now can we go and see my horse?" asked Dewi.

"Come on," said the man.

With a ringing of boots on the flagstones, and a chiming of young voices, he and the children and Harry the dog clattered out of the cottage and Delia was alone. She stacked the dishes and carried them out to the scullery, fetched water from the well, refilled the kettle and put it on the fire for washing up. While the water boiled she swept up the hearth and chopped some kindling for the morning and while she worked she sang, a smooth piping wordless song like a bird's. What she was doing was just the usual routine of a woman's labour but it seemed different tonight, it had a magic. Silver and gold. It was growing dark but the cottage seemed full of light and she had an unexplainable sensation of having come into a fortune.

5

IT WAS EARLY when she woke next morning and at first she thought she was at home, for the sun was shining full on the chest her father had made and carved with the two herons, and stretched over herself and Megan was the patchwork quilt. She sat up and looked about her at unfamiliar things, a ewer and basin, a tallboy and a mirror on the wall, and knew where she was, but she did not lose her sense of being at home. She got up, washed and dressed quickly and went out into the garden. The mist had nearly vanished but the garden was spun all over with dewdrops and spiders' webs. She walked through the apple trees and tiger lilies and came to the gateway and there she stood and looked out over the valley towards the hills and the blue break in them that led to the Bay of the Seals. How was it that a particular scene, or creatures like the herons, could belong to this world and yet seem not of it but of that other one?

She asked the question silently in her mind and then she asked it aloud because he had come and was standing beside her. "You make your own world," he said. "You take to yourself certain things that belong to you, certain places and creatures, certain people. Some person, even some scene you see only once may be of your world and will be with you till you die."

"And do we take our own world with us when we die?" she asked.

He laughed. "How should I know? Perhaps, if you love it enough to have it inside you. Now what on earth did you mean by asking me if I had bought your mother's things?"

"My great grandmother made the patchwork quilt I slept under last night, and my father made the chest with the herons on it. Some of your lustre jugs were my mother's. After she died I had to sell them to The Shop in Trawscoed."

He looked round in astonishment. "Yes, I bought them. In the outside world that would be called a coincidence. In this world, this inside one, it might have another name. Especially as it's doubled. I have your things and you have mine. You have stolen, I mean come by, my stolen horse."

It was Delia's turn to look round in astonishment. They were facing each other now, looking into each other's faces. "The silver horse? Does Dewi know it's yours?"

"I hadn't the heart to tell him. It's his, you see, by virtue of love, for he knows Silver by heart as thoroughly as I know the patches on your quilt. He can no more be parted from my horse than I can from your quilt. So now what do we do?"

Not knowing the answer Delia ignored the question. "So when Silver brought us here," she said, "he was just coming home to his own stable."

"The stable he prefers," said the man. "We've two homes, Silver and I. There's a big one, damnably cold and desolate, out there," and he gestured beyond the valley, "and this one, my farm and my hide-out, in our private world."

"Do you go often to the home in the outside world?" asked Delia.

"Not as often as I should," he said, and though he did not take his eyes from hers he crimsoned with a sort of shame. "That damned bailiff does things without my knowledge. Yet how can I blame the fellow if I take no interest in what he does? Forgive me, Delia."

"Forgive you?"

"That you were turned out of your cottage. I was short of money, I always am, it's those damned races and the cards, and I told him to put the pressure on somewhere. He did, on you. I didn't know it was you. I didn't bother to know. Please forgive me."

Delia gazed at him in astonishment, and then slowly she understood and the colour rushed into her face too, then ebbed, leaving her so white that he took hold of her elbow. "You're the squire," she said.

"Do you hate me?" he asked.

"No."

"Though I get into debt, and my horse stops at every pub, and I am the worst squire in the Principality? Why don't you hate me?"

"You didn't tell Dewi the silver horse isn't his horse."

"You haven't answered my other question, Delia."

"What question?"

"What do we do? About Silver? About my being such a bad squire? About everything?"

"I don't know," she said.

"Are you very brave?" he asked. "Well, of course you are.

But are you reckless? Are you reckless enough to marry me?"

"Marry you?" gasped Delia, and she grew whiter still, so that he tightened his grip on her elbow.

"About this private world," he said. "If we say goodbye today and I never see you again you'll be in mine until I die. Will I be in yours?"

Delia, speechless, nodded. A voice inside her said, "And after I die," but it only spoke inside her.

"Then wouldn't it be a pity to say goodbye today? And what do we do about that quilt? I'm not parting with it."

Delia looked away from him for a moment, over the sunlit valley to the hills and the sea. It was a landscape of joy, and joy sparkled on all the myriad crystalline spiders' webs. "Oh look!" she cried. They had stood still so long that a busy spider had tied them together with a shining rope. When they laughed and clung to each other they broke it in the world of time but in no other world.

Three Men

Three Men

ST GABRIEL'S CHAPEL was built in a fissure of the rocks, facing the sea. No one knew its age. There was a legend, but who can believe legends? It was said that one Christmas Eve centuries ago the sole survivor of a shipwreck had crawled up the gully and found shelter from the storm a floor of white sand and a spring of fresh water. Here he had slaked his thirst and here in the morning fishermen had found him, insensible but still alive. He had recovered and in gratitude had built St. Gabriel's Chapel, with a hermitage attached to it, and lived out the rest of his life there, thanking God that he had not died that night in his faithlessness and sin but had been granted time for penitence, and the opening of his eyes to the truths of the Christian faith. While he lived, at his request, one of the monks from the neighbouring monastery had said mass in the chapel on the anniversary of his escape, and the country folk had loved to come and worship with him on Christmas Eve, and on his deathbed he had asked the monks to continue the practice for ever. If they would do so, he said, the spring of fresh water would never fail, and it would be holy water that would open the eyes of the blind. And there would always be a congregation, he had promised, even if it was only three men. The congregation would never fail the celebrant.

"But it will tonight," muttered Father Ambrose, digging his heels into the plump sides of Tobias the monastery ass. "Now get on, Tobias. Confound the beast! It would have been better to walk."

Tobias thought it would have been better to stay at home. He did not know what they were doing out here on the moor in the snow. He was getting old and the weight on his back was considerable, for Father Ambrose was a large man. Tobias straddled his legs out and stood still.

The old monk groaned, and a few tears of self-pity welled up in his rheumy old eyes. Every Christmas the monks cast lots as to who should go to St. Gabriel's and in his younger days the lot had never fallen on him. But now, in his old age, it had. Father Abbot should have forbidden him to go, for he knew how blind he was with this cataract growing over his eyes, and how rheumatic. Father Abbot was a hard man. How strange it was that these hard men were so often sentimentalists, for surely it was sentimental to insist, as Father Abbot insisted, that year after year this ancient custom must be carried on. Father Ambrose was tonight convinced, though he had not thought so before, that it should now be allowed to lapse. It was said that the continuity had never been broken but that could hardly be true. During those years when the monks had been driven from their monastery it must have been broken. There was, of course, that other legend, but who can believe legends?

It was said that not all the monks had left the neighbourhood when the monastery had been dissolved. One young monk had taken refuge in the oak forest that bordered the moor to the north, built himself a hut in a deep hollow of the woods and lived there as a wood-cutter. He had lived to a great age and he had never failed to say mass in the chapel on Christmas Eve. What had happened during the years after his death, until the monks came back again, was not known, but it was said there had always been some priest who secretly came, and a congregation too, even if it was only three men.

"And I should be ashamed that I've no wish to do my duty this night," said Father Ambrose, suddenly contrite, and he lowered himself painfully to the ground. He must walk, dragging the donkey and carrying the lantern, with the sacred vessels, the candles and his vestments a dead weight in the leather bag that

was slung round his shoulders. Tobias was quite willing to go
on if dragged. It was fat men on his back that he objected to.

Father Ambrose found it hard going, even though he was in the
lee of the oak wood, and he thought that he would repeat some
holy words to keep his exhaustion at bay.

" 'Whither shall I go then from thy spirit? or whither shall
I go then from thy presence?

'If I climb up into heaven, thou art there; if I go down to hell,
thou art there also.

'If I take the wings of the morning, and remain in the uttermost parts of the sea:

'Even there also shall thy hand lead me, and thy right hand
shall hold me.

'If I say, Peradventure the darkness shall cover me: then shall
my night be turned to day'."

But his night was very far from being turned to day and he
missed the path when it left the wood and turned across the
moor to the chapel. He wondered what to do. He could follow
the wood-shore to the edge of the cliff but it would take him a
mile or so out of his way and he would reach the chapel long
after midnight. Yet that, he decided, was what he must do, and
he staggered forward again.

But he had gone only a short way when the lantern showed him
an opening like a doorway in the wall of the wood beside him.
To his dim sight its blackness gaped horribly, as though it were
a passage leading down into hell. Out of it came footprints,
brown and earthy in the snow as though freshly made by some
beast who had his lair in the deeps of the earth, or by some
savage man of the woods who had wrapped his feet in rags to
ease the cold. Father Ambrose stood still and he was afraid. He
dared not go on. He might even have gone back had it not been
for Tobias, who recovering suddenly from his obstinacy moved
forward and plodded off to the left in the track of the footprints.

"Confound the ass! Tobias, wait for me!" cried Father Ambrose,
and stumbling after the donkey he scrambled on his back again
and they went on together. The wind, now that they were away
from the wood, was cruel, but Father Ambrose was no longer
afraid; or rather he was not afraid until Tobias stopped again,
his head hanging, and lowering the lantern he saw that the
earthy footprints were lost. The snow had covered them. Then

indeed the old man was in despair and groaned to God to help him.

He sat on the donkey's back shivering and weeping and so savage was the wind that it whirled the snow in the air and made a sort of swinging spiral staircase of it, a stairway so high and dreadful that it seemed to climb up into heaven. Then the snow was like wings in the sky and it seemed as though one ran upon the stairs, ran down lightly and quickly, though his stature was greater than that of a man. The snow wings folded and as they folded the wind dropped a little and Tobias lifted his head and went forward again, stepping with a sudden lightness as though he had forgotten his fatigue. Father Ambrose, peering down, dimly saw that footprints had appeared once more. They were larger than before and had a new shapeliness. They were no longer earthy and the lantern light filled them with gold.

Quite soon Father Ambrose heard the booming of the sea. He also saw to his joy that a few stars were shining in the rents of the clouds and presently a full moon sailed into a pool of clear sky. The storm was passing and in no time at all, it seemed, he had slipped from Tobias's back and was leading him down into the gully. Below him was St. Gabriel's, so old that it looked like a storm-beaten rock, and beside him the spring bubbled up into its basin of stone. Here he was sheltered from the wind and it seemed to him as warm as spring. But his eyes were still painful and burning from the cold and kneeling beside the spring he laved them in the water. Then he went round to the door of the chapel that faced the shore. Here he tethered Tobias to a ring in the wall, set his lantern down beside the door and before going inside turned to look out across the sea.

It roared below him, but the peak of the storm was passed and the tide going out. More and more stars blazed in the heavens and the moon was so bright that he could see the rock pools reflecting the stars, and the round wet pebbles of the beach. The night was as clear as the day and everything he saw sharp-edged and beautiful as in his clear-sighted boyhood . . . He was no longer half-blind . . . He knelt down on the path and thanked God.

Still kneeling, he thought how clear the footprints were, coming up from the sea. The moonlight filled each one, brimming it with silver. This was the third time he had seen footprints. Awe fell upon him, and when he got up and turned round to face the chapel door again his knees were trembling, for the footprints went right up to the door, as though the man from the uttermost parts of the sea had gone inside. He conquered his trembling, took up his lantern and followed. Tobias jerked the rusty ring to which he was tethered out of the wall and followed him, standing just inside the chapel door.

Father Ambrose walked to the rough stone altar and set down his lantern. The little place was low and arched like a cave and he remembered that men said the stable at Bethlehem, to which Gabriel had directed the shepherds, had been a cave . . . Gabriel . . . Whether there was a congregation behind him in the shadows he did not know for he had kept his eyes on the ground when he entered this holy place. He lifted the heavy leather bag from his shoulders and took out the candles, put them on the altar and lighted them. He vested and set out the sacred vessels. About the hour of midnight, by the light of moon and candles, he said mass, and during the responses he heard voices in the sound of the sea. The Gloria rose like a wave and crashed in a deep mutter of sound. When the time came for the congregation to approach the altar there were three. He did not see them for tears were running down his face. He wept for his unworthiness. He wept also for joy. When, at the end of mass, his thanksgiving said, he turned round, his sight was still that of a boy of twelve but only the donkey was there. He went out, mounted Tobias and rode home singing the 139th psalm very much off key.

When Father Abbot asked him if there had been a congregation he said briefly, yes, there had been the three men . . . Or two men and one other . . . Father Abbot forbore to ask him what he meant for he perceived that the man who had ridden back to the monastery was not quite the same man who had ridden out.

Father Ambrose lived to a great old age, clear-sighted in more ways than one until the end.

Lost — One Angel

Lost — One Angel

I

THE YOUNGEST ANGEL was fed up. At five years old he had never really understood what the Nativity play was all about, though plenty of people had done their best to explain it to him, and the rehearsals had wearied him beyond endurance. The angels wore their wings at rehearsals, to get used to them, and his had nearly sent him crackers. The other children's wings stayed put fairly well but his were always twisting crooked or falling off, and he was in perpetual trouble with authority because when a lamb was put into his arms and he was thrust down to kneel in adoration at the foot of the manger he wouldn't adore. Why should he? It was only a doll in the manger and they had a real baby at home. He couldn't see the sense in it, and when it came to the dress rehearsal and he was dressed in a white frock like a girl's, and his newly-washed yellow curls were fluffed out and he was made to look a fool, he decided to quit, and did so just before the scene where he had to kneel with the lamb in his arms and gaze at the china thing as though he liked it. How could he like it when they had a real baby at home? They ought to see the baby up at his place and then they'd see the fools they were to make such a fuss over a thing like that. Full of powerful indignation he roamed round to the back of the stage where it was dark, threw the lamb in a corner, pushed open a door and went out. No one saw him go.

It startled him, when he came out, to find it was daylight still, for in the church hall where the rehearsal was taking place they had darkened the windows to rehearse the lighting. His surroundings were unfamiliar to him, for until today they had rehearsed the play at school. He stood in an asphalted yard. To one side of him there was a big church and in front was an archway in a wall and beyond that was the roar of London on the day before Christmas Eve. He went to the archway and stood there at the top of a flight of steps, looking down at the hurrying people below. He was quite warm for though it was a day with only an occasional gleam of sun it was not cold and he had his winter vest on, and his pants and his new Wellingtons. He had refused to take his boots off and go barefoot like the other angels and as he was such a difficult boy just at present authority had not pressed him, for fear of yells. They hoped he would be more amenable on the night, which was Boxing Day. Everyone understood why he was difficult just now. It was the new baby. He was immensely proud of it but for five years his reign had been sole and undisputed and he could not quite understand the present divided allegiance. And while his mother had been at the hospital he had been sent to stay with Gran, a disciplinarian of the old school, and had suffered much, if deservedly. His small world had been shaken to its foundations and he was much confused.

Where, now, were home and Mum? To the right or the left? He thought, as it happened inaccurately, that they were to the right, and decided he would go down. Step by step he descended, winged and glowing, like Gabriel coming down from heaven with his good tidings of great joy.

Once down on the pavement he trudged purposefully along, his wings crooked as usual and his celestial robe lifted on each side to show his Wellingtons. He aroused a certain amount of curiosity and amusement but no concern, for he appeared to know where he was going and to be happy and content. But when he had passed by he was not forgotten, for his hair was very yellow and his eyes most deeply blue. Some hearts ached at his passing while others leaped with a sense of expectancy. But some people were too self-engrossed, or in too much of a hurry, to notice him at all. They wouldn't have noticed God himself if they'd happened to collide with him on the pavement. These pushed and shoved the small angel and once or twice he nearly fell down, but he went doggedly on and gave no sign of the mounting panic in his heart. Once or twice he whispered, "Mum, Mum," but even when he knew he was lost he did not cry. He was a brave little boy.

2

MRS. RODNEY GLANCED at the Dresden clock on her mantelpiece and found to her despair that she had fifteen minutes to wait. Her taxi was ordered, her luggage already packed and downstairs, and she had nothing to do. She sat down in front of her empty grate and stared at it. Her service flat was centrally heated but she usually had a small wood fire burning just for the look of the thing. Today, as she was catching an afternoon train to spend Christmas at Brighton, there was only dead ash in the pretty basket grate and it depressed her dreadfully. She was a woman of over sixty but so marvellously groomed that she did not look her age. She had divorced her husband years ago and she had no children. She was well-off and when the immaculate beauty of her flat became intolerable she travelled. She had very painful arthritis, though she kept it at bay with the latest treatments. She never spoke of her arthritis to anyone because though she had many acquaintances whose parties she attended, and for whom she gave parties in return, she had no real friends. Beneath her accomplished social charm she was a shy woman, and the shining armour that she wore herself intimidated her when she confronted it in others. And everyone she knew seemed to wear it. If shut away inside themselves they were as lonely and scared as she was they gave no sign.

She glanced again at the clock. Ten more minutes. Why should she feel despairing just because she had to wait a few minutes for a taxi, and there was only dead ash in the grate? Nowadays the smallest thing seemed to open up a sort of dry hopelessness within her. And today she was particularly vulnerable because of that dream.

She had dreamed she was back in her childhood, a small girl gazing in ecstasy at the Christmas angel on top of the tree. He was a ridiculous cherub with pink cheeks and yellow hair, made of sawdust and china, with a celestial robe of butter muslin and

D

wings of cotton wool. She thought he was wonderful. The tree was blazing with candles and on it hung presents for them all, but the only thing she wanted was the little angel. The other children were laughing and chattering and pointing at the tree, and the candlelight was reflected in their eyes. Their father was opening his penknife with maddening deliberation, ready to cut their presents from the branches. She was the youngest and she was standing next to their mother, so near that her small hand stole among the soft folds of her mother's dress and she could bury her nose in the bunch of violets that was tucked into her belt. The waits were singing carols outside in the street. Her mother's hand, that had been lying on her shoulder, lifted and caressed her cheek. Then the dream began to pass and she found herself standing back from it all, looking on. She watched the children and their parents, and above all she watched the little girl who was herself. She saw how she leaned her cheek against her mother's hand, and how she gazed up at the little angel at the top of the tree. Then abruptly the scene was blotted out by darkness and she cried out and woke up and remembered that they were all dead.

The dream had haunted her through the day, and above all she had been haunted by the Christmas angel, lost and broken long ago. He seemed to stand for all the lost bliss of childhood, as the empty grate with its grey ashes stood for the present dereliction of her days. Dereliction? What a ridiculous word to use. And she was not sure if she even knew what it meant. It would do her good to spend Christmas at the Brighton hotel. There would be crowds about her and she would have no time to brood.

The hall porter rang through to say the taxi was there and she slipped into her fur coat, that was soft and light as though made of thistledown. Glancing at herself in the mirror over the fireplace she saw a tall slender woman with a delicately tinted face that looked oddly mask-like. As she left her flat and crossed to the lift she asked herself, what else could one do? To wear this mask of beauty was the only form of courage that she knew.

Downstairs Parks, the porter, was already putting her cases in the taxi. When he saw her come out he opened the door of the taxi and stood at attention, his hand to his peaked cap, smiling at her with kindly deference. He had beautiful manners and always made her feel she was somebody still. Very different from the taxi driver, lolling back in his seat with a cigarette dangling from the corner of his mouth. As she crossed the pavement his eyes flicked over her, as though calculating the cost of her pearls and her fur coat. She got in and Parks closed the door gently and tenderly upon her, as though she were something indescribably fragile and precious. She leaned back and then feeling that she would like to wish Parks a happy Christmas she leaned forward again, and just caught the contemptuous wink that he exchanged with the taxi driver.

Somehow it hurt her intolerably to discover that Parks was not what he had always seemed. She supposed he was a socialist, like all the rest. Perhaps he was a communist. She was sure the taxi driver was and an irrational pang of fear went through her. She sat and looked at the jaunty set of his cap and the bristles of hair in the back of his neck, as a short while before she had been looking at her empty grate, and she disliked him intensely.

After a few turnings she saw the beacon of a Belisha crossing ahead and suddenly there was a grinding of brakes all about them and they stopped. The momentary check vexed her. How tiresome it was! At least those wretched pedestrians might have the courtesy to pass quickly and not keep a whole block of traffic waiting interminably like this. Her driver, with no train to catch, was leaning back indolently, uninterested in whoever it might be who was holding them up, but Mrs. Rodney in her exasperation let down her window and looked out, to become instantly aware that almost everyone except her driver was also looking out, or else down from the tops of the buses. Something or someone upon the Belisha crossing was holding them enchanted. For a moment, so unlike herself was she today, she thought the whole of London was waiting and watching, the silence was so extraordinary. Standing up she leaned right out, and with her height was able to see over the low sports car and the errand boys in front of her and get a clear view of the crossing.

The sun had just struggled out through the grey clouds and in a nimbus of glory a small angel was drifting slowly across the street, the traffic banked up on either side of him like the waters of the Nile when the Israelites crossed over. An angel in London. An angel on a Belisha crossing. Most people could hardly believe the evidence of their own eyes but Mrs. Rodney instantly recognized him. It was her own angel of whom she had dreamed last night. She could not mistake the little white robe, the fluffy wings, the yellow curls and rosy cheeks. In the charmed silence her conviction seemed to reach to all in the crowd about her and to them too, as their first stunned astonishment passed, he was their own, something lost, something hoped for, something cradled and adored within them. But no one moved or spoke until suddenly the indolent taxi driver caught sight of the heavenly vision. He let out a yell. "My God, it's our Ernie!" The angel passed over, the traffic reared forward again and the quiet moment was swept away as though it had never been.

Beyond the crossing the taxi jolted to a standstill beside the curb, the driver jumped out and wrenched the door open. "Sorry, lady, I must leave you," he said abruptly. "That was my kid and I must catch him."

"Mine too," said Mrs. Rodney. "I'll help you." And leaving her beautiful pigskin cases unguarded in the taxi she ran with the driver back to the Belisha crossing, and scarcely felt her arthritis. His hand gripping her elbow they crossed over. She did think just for a fleeting moment that she must have gone mad and then in the excitement of the chase she forgot about it. "You go one way and I'll go the other," she gasped breathlessly. "Ask people if they've seen him. He can't have gone far. We'll meet here again."

Half an hour later they met again at the beacon and they had not found Ernie. Mrs. Rodney looked at the driver. His face was white and beads of sweat stood on his upper lip. He was a man of about forty and very ordinary. There was nothing to distinguish him from a thousand others and Mrs. Rodney herself would not have noticed him at all had it not been for their mutual concern for a treasure lost, a concern which in his case was turning into anguish. She saw the misery in his eyes and she saw something else, an experience of life and suffering of which she had never known, and never would know anything at all. She reflected that he was of an age to have served in the war. She also reflected that she herself had spent the war in a comfortable hotel at Torquay. Such reflections were unlike her but she was not herself today. He began to speak quickly and breathlessly.

"Ernie, he's in a play the kids are rehearsing at the church hall this afternoon. Nativity play, they call it. Ernie's an angel. Fed up with it, he is. He's cut and run. But where does he think he's running to? Why didn't he go home? He's in a mood just now is Ernie. The wife's just had a new one and Ernie don't understand it. Been the only pebble on the beach for too long and his mum and I proper took up with him. The wife's not strong yet."

His voice suddenly snapped off and Mrs. Rodney realised that he was in too much distress to know what to do. "We must go back to the taxi and drive to the nearest police station," she said. "A lost angel is a matter for the police I think."

They went back to the taxi, where she never even noticed that her luggage was still miraculously safe, and drove through side streets at breakneck speed to the police station. They went in together, such an oddly assorted couple that the portly sergeant's mouth twitched with amusement as Mrs. Rodney explained the situation. He had had a couple a short while before and in spite of the anxiety of the man before him the humour of the situation was more apparent to him than its potential tragedy. He adjusted his spectacles, drew a sheet of paper towards him and wrote at its head, in a large flowing hand, 'Lost—One Angel'. He underlined this statement and then asked for particulars. The driver gave them steadily, his name, Bert Thomas, his address and a description of the child.

"Keep your chin up, mate," said the sergeant. "I'll alert the stations and put this statement on the notice board. You'll have the boy back by night, I shouldn't wonder. Bye-bye."

Mrs. Rodney and Bert went back to the taxi. "Your train, ma'am!" he cried, suddenly aghast.

"It does not matter," she said. "I have changed my mind. I do not think I will leave town for Christmas after all. Will you take me back again to my flat?"

They drove back to their starting point and now it was Bert, not Parks, who hurried to open the door of the taxi and heave out the luggage. "Thank you, ma'am," he said simply.

"I hope Ernie will be none the worse for his adventure," said Mrs. Rodney. "You'll soon find him, I know. Goodbye, Mr. Thomas. A happy Christmas to you."

She went upstairs to her flat and did not even notice the dead ash in the grate. She had carefully memorised Bert's address and now she wrote it down in her address book. She knew the angel would soon be found but she would go round tomorrow just to make sure. Would they mind if she took a Christmas present for him and for the baby? She did not think they would mind. What should she take? Trying to decide between this thing and the other kept her pleasantly employed for the rest of the evening and that abyss of hopelessness did not once open within her.

3

THERE WAS A Belisha crossing near Ernie's home and when he saw the orange beacon looming up above him his heart gave a leap of joy. He had been feeling dreadfully tired and miserable, and now he was home. But when he had crossed over to the other side he wasn't where he had thought he would be. Yet still he did not cry. He had inherited a great deal of grit from his father and although any frustration of his will made him howl and roar, when things were really bad he was silent.

He turned right and went doggedly on for a couple of minutes until from sheer exhaustion he stumbled and went down on hands and knees. Scrambling up again he turned sideways and there in front of him was a flight of steps. He was back again, he thought, at the place where they were doing the play. It was not home but it was the next best thing. He would not mind being in the play any more now. He climbed up the steps, blind with fatigue, not noticing what was at the top, and went through the wide swing doors, that a few minutes before had been hooked back to allow some luggage to be carried out. Inside was a warm dim sort of cavern so thickly carpeted that the man who was sorting letters inside a glass cubicle to the left did not hear Ernie enter, and he did not see the yellow head so far below the level of his eyes. In front of Ernie, at the back of the cavern, was an oblong of light, the shape of a door. He stumbled towards it and it wasn't a door but an empty box full of light set up on end. He stumbled in and collapsed in a corner. It was warm and quiet and above him in the box was a lamp like a star. He fell asleep and the star shone down on him.

4

COLONEL ANSTRUTHER WALKED slowly down the sunny side of the street, even though the sun was not out, just in case it should come out. It was on the whole a rather gloomy day but there were occasional gleams of sunshine. There had been one five minutes ago, fleeting but so lovely that he had stopped and taken his hat off. People had stared at him but he was used to that. He had lived so long and was now so outmoded that people invariably looked at him as though he had strayed out of Madame Tussaud's. It had been such a golden gleam, so gay and reassuring, so tender and amused. It had seemed to bring a profound silence with it, as though all the traffic in London had suddenly been halted, and in the silence he had thought he heard light footsteps running, like the footsteps of a rescuing Child. It was then he had taken his hat off. Then he realised that the silence had been within himself and when he looked about him he could see no child.

He walked slowly on again, very erect in spite of his age, his left hand behind him in the small of his back and his right hand manipulating his walking stick with a slow grace. He was very clean and neat and his clothes had been well made, though they were old and worn now. He wore his hat at an elegant angle and he always had a flower in his buttonhole. He had piercing blue eyes and a snow-white walrus moustache, thought to be the last in London. He lived in lodgings somewhere but it was suspected that they were not very comfortable because he spent a great deal of time at his club, which with the flower in his buttonhole appeared to be his one luxury, for he never took a holiday or went to the theatre. He never talked about himself but it was known he had served in India and in the first world war, and on Remembrance Sunday he appeared with an imposing array of medals on his breast. It was very much feared that he had no income but his pension, adequate years ago but not now. No one knew him very well because his particular brand of integrity would allow him to make no claim upon the compassion of others, and as his need for it grew so did his reserve. But his courtesy never failed. It was slightly impersonal, and as old-fashioned as his hat, but untarnishable.

The police station was on the sunny side of the street and he passed it every day without much notice of it, but today a painful breathlessness from which he sometimes suffered came upon him just as he was walking by, and to hide his distress from others he turned towards the notice board. There was a railing beside it which he was able to hold with his free hand. He was better presently, and able to let go of the railing and wipe his forehead with his old silk handkerchief. His sight, still so good that he only needed glasses for small print, cleared again and he was able to bring the notice board into focus. 'Lost—One Angel.'

Colonel Anstruther was so astonished that he thought he must be making a mistake, and put on his spectacles. Yes, an angel. He read the particulars carefully, registering the address of the child's home in his retentive memory, and was very greatly distressed. Half a lifetime ago he had lost first a small son and then a young wife in India and the loss had left him with a shy yet passionate love for all young children and their mothers. That a mother should be weeping for a lost son at Christmas was to him the very height of tragedy for it was one that he had himself witnessed and endured. He walked on down the street, at first very sadly, and then he endeavoured to turn his thoughts to hope. He did not consider himself a man of prayer but with all the strength that he had he desired and believed that the footsteps of the boy should at this moment turn inwards to a place of safety.

Twenty minutes later he reached his club and paused beside the porter's cubicle in the vestibule to ask if there were any letters for him. He thought there might be as it was Christmas. But there was nothing, not even a card. He reminded himself that there were few people left alive now to remember him. "They are all gone into the world of light," he quoted to himself. He thought that he would go to the library and read for a while, for there was no one about to speak to and the club seemed deserted. He would have liked to have ordered himself a cup of tea but he did not have afternoon tea nowadays. It cost too much.

The lift was beside the library door but as he walked towards it he did not recognize the oblong of light confronting him. He was still a little confused after the queer turn he had had in the street. It looked like a lighted porch leading to unimaginable glory. "The world of light," he murmured to himself, and he thought he would go in. But at the threshold of the porch he was brought up abruptly, for there was an angel curled up asleep in the corner. A very small one. The starry light overhead shone down upon the yellow head and fluffy crumpled white wings. The round cheeks were flushed with sleep and the long curved lashes

lying on them were delicate as gossamer. The shock was so great
that Colonel Anstruther was taken again with that rather painful
breathlessness. But this time he soon felt better, and the first
thing he noted upon recovery was a stout little pair of Wellingtons
protruding from beneath the celestial robe. The situation was
then clear to him and he went over to the porter's cubicle and
said, "Jackson, there's an angel in the lift. I shall be obliged
if you will call me a taxi."

Jackson had feared for some time that old Colonel Anstruther
was getting a little muddled in his head. His fear now crystallized
into certainty. "I'll see to it, sir," he said soothingly, and
advanced with slow majesty upon the lift. "Cor!" he ejaculated,
coming to an abrupt halt.

"Don't wake him," said Colonel Anstruther. "Call me a taxi
and I'll take him to the police station. As I passed I saw on the
notice board that there's an angel lost." His voice took on a note
of military precision. "Don't stand staring, Jackson. Have you
never seen an angel before? Call me a taxi at once."

Jackson did so, and then carried out the sleeping Ernie and
put him on the old gentleman's knees in the cab. "Nice little
chap," he murmured, and having given the taxi driver his
instructions he lingered on the pavement to watch them drive
away. He had had Ernie in his arms for such a short while but
he would not forget it.

Nor would Colonel Anstruther forget it. The boy was a very
solid weight upon his frail knees but he scarcely noticed it.
Ernie, half awake but entirely contented now that the atmosphere
of extreme devotion to which he was accustomed once more
enfolded him, leaned his yellow head with royal condescension
against the old man's shoulder and automatically appropriated
the flower in his buttonhole. Colonel Anstruther had forgotten
that the hair of a clean and healthy child is delicately fragrant.
The scent came back to him over the years with very great
poignancy, and it made the child in his arms seem peculiarly
his own. It was with anguish that he realized that the taxi had
stopped and their time together was over. But he gave no sign
of emotion and abruptly refusing the taxi driver's offer to carry
the little chap, for he looked an 'eavy lump, he took Ernie inside
and handed him over to a portly sergeant, who received him
into his arms with as much delight as though he were his own

grandson. "One angel—found," he ejaculated, and pinched Ernie's cheek with much appreciation. Colonel Anstruther, having ascertained that a police officer would take Ernie instantly to his home in the waiting taxi, refused somewhat haughtily to give his name and address, walked out of the police station and back to his club.

Sitting in the library he felt so tired that he thought he would order himself a pot of tea after all. He couldn't afford it, but it was Christmas. Sipping the hot reviving stuff, and holding the cup in both his thin blue-veined hands because they were trembling slightly after the exertion of carrying Ernie, he realized suddenly that he could not part with the boy. To do so would be like shutting the window in the face of spring. What could he do? The only thing he could think of was that tomorrow, Christmas Eve, he should buy some little gift for the child and take it round. He remembered the address but lest he forget it he took out his notebook and jotted it down. If he were to give up smoking for a month he could get the little chap quite a nice gift. He spent a happy half-hour, the happiest for years, sipping his tea and wondering what it should be.

5

CHRISTMAS EVE WAS clear and blue, and not even the glaring lights of London could quite extinguish the far gleam of the stars. Bert was off duty tonight, and a succulent tea of kippers and buttered toast was just drawing to a greasy but satisfactory conclusion; that is as far as he and Ernie were concerned, Vera his wife had finished some while ago and was sitting by the fire feeding Roy the baby. He was a strong and healthy child with a great deal of fair fluff on the top of his head, imperious manners and a very powerful gift of self-expression. The moments when he was engaged in nourishing himself were much valued for their peace.

Bert lit a cigarette and sat back contentedly. It was warm and comfortable in the kitchen and Vera, the firelight on her face, was looking as pretty as ever he'd seen her. Ernie was beside him, topping off with chocolate. He thought to himself that it needed a jolt such as he had had yesterday to make a man appreciate his luck. He wished he knew who the old boy was who had found Ernie. He'd like to thank him. It was hard not to know who he was.

A rather authoritative knock came at the front door. "It'll be Mum," said Vera, and Bert rose with resignation, for it was Vera's mother, not his, whom they were expecting.

But it was not Mum's downright tones that Vera heard when Bert opened the front door at the end of the passage, but a voice sweet and clear and slightly affected, as ladies' voices mostly were in Vera's opinion. Vera herself was an intensely loving woman but as downright as her mother. Bert, to her horror, was asking the lady to step inside, and for a moment of sheer panic she thought he was going to bring her straight into the kitchen. Then with relief she heard the click of the door of the front room. He'd had that much sense, she thanked God. You never knew with Bert.

Her husband's head came round the door. "It's the old gal who lent me a hand yesterday," he said. "I told you. Wants to see you an' Ernie and the baby. Bring 'em along, Vera."

"I'm feeding Roy," said Vera coldly.

"It don't matter," said Bert. "Come as you are, Roy an' all. She's a married woman and a decent old gal." Then meeting his wife's steely gaze he realized that this was one of the occasions when she was taking after her mother. "Come when you can then," he temporized. "I'll take Ernie."

"He's all over chocolate and kipper," said Vera. "The dishcloth's by the sink."

Bert polished up Ernie and hauled him off and presently Vera, listening intently, heard above the hum of conversation in the next room another knock on the front door, not authoritative this time but humble. Who was it? She did not know but her heart stirred with a strange sense of welcome and she was in a panic because Bert had apparently not heard the knock. Then it came again, low and gentle, and this time Bert did hear and went to the door. The voice she heard then, so quietly courteous, was one she had somehow been expecting. She had been feeling exasperated but now she felt at peace, and looked down lovingly at the boy at her breast. What was it about him? He was quite an ordinary baby yet people were perpetually coming in and out to see him. It was partly Ernie's doing, of course, always talking about the new baby, but it wasn't only that. She supposed it was because he was new-born just at this time. Christmas set a light about him.

Roy had finished his meal and was now at his best, satisfied, pink, sleepy, silent. She wrapped him in his shawl and took him in the crook of her arm. She was not nervous as she went down the passage for an odd sense of assurance came to her, as though she were a queen. She opened the door and came in smiling, and when she had sat down in the chair that the old gentleman quickly vacated for her she opened the shawl and showed them the baby with a dignity and sweetness that Bert never afterwards forgot.

Ernie behaved beautifully. Clasping to his chest the woolly lamb that Mrs. Rodney had just given him, though he didn't care about it as much as Colonel Anstruther's model aeroplane, he kneeled down beside his mother and gazed at Roy with angelic and selfless adoration. It was a histrionic reflex action, for the woolly lamb was just like the silly thing they'd thrust into his arms during rehearsals, when they'd told him to look and smile and love the baby, and he wouldn't, it being china, but it touched Mrs. Rodney so much that she had to dive into her bag for a handkerchief. She recovered herself in a moment and was eloquent in admiration of Ernie and the baby. While Bert answered her Vera looked up at the tall old man beside her. Their eyes met and she knew that he understood her love for her baby as no one else did, or ever would do, not even Bert.

6

THE DOOR HAD shut behind them and Mrs. Rodney and Colonel Anstruther were alone together in the dingy street. The goodbyes of Bert and Vera had been affectionate and they had been invited to come again and had said they would, so they had no reason to feel shut out. Yet they both suddenly felt lonely and old. The roar of London had an impersonal sound and though the stars were not obliterated by the neon lights it was not very easy to see them.

"I have a taxi waiting," said Mrs. Rodney charmingly. "May I drop you anywhere? I live in Chelsea."

"I shall be most grateful for the kindness," said Colonel Anstruther. He did not feel very easy with her, and the scent of her luxurious soft fur coat and of her perfume oppressed him a little, but he was very tired and he would be glad not to have to struggle home by bus. They walked together to the car, not a taxi at all but a hired Daimler that she occasionally used, and he handed her in and sat beside her. "Anywhere near Chelsea gardens, if you will be so good," he said. From there it would not be too far for him to walk to his lodgings. A quirk of pride made him unwilling that she should actually see where he lived.

Their progress was slow for there were so many cars and buses crowding the streets, so many Christmas shoppers jamming the pavements and the crossings. At first Mrs. Rodney talked brightly of the charm of the little family they had left, and then of whatever else she could think of as a topic of conversation, and Colonel Anstruther did his courteous best to make appropriate replies. But once they had finished with Bert and his family he did not always quite know how to answer for he never went to the Riviera these days, nor to the ballet or the Academy. And so gradually little silences came between them in which both began to be aware of the familiar swaying, tumbling, surging brilliance of the London night sky and the London night streets. They took on added enchantment on Christmas Eve for as the shop windows flashed by there were half-glimpsed tinsel stars and spangled angels, lighted Christmas trees and bunches of holly. The people surging along the pavements were excited and happy, and among them were a great many bright-eyed children clutching parcels done up in coloured paper. The familiar hot petrol stench of dried-up London came in through the windows freshened by the scent of oranges and greenery, and, now and again, flowers. Mrs. Rodney found it all very moving tonight. Colonel Anstruther saw it as though it was a curtain swaying in the wind, or a passing dream. What was real to him was the picture of Vera looking up at him, and understanding that he understood. The whole of London seemed only to exist tonight because of Vera with Roy in her arms.

The car swung away from the busy streets and glided down a quieter one towards the river, and again came the scent of flowers. Colonel Anstruther spoke to the chauffeur through the speaking tube, and when the car stopped he murmured a word of apology to Mrs. Rodney and got out and went into the flower shop. Inside he bought a bunch of violets and coming back to the car again he gave them to her, courteously wishing her a happy Christmas. Behind her laughing chatter and the make-up on her face he had been from the beginning aware of great desolation but also of a matching courage Though he did not feel at ease with this woman he could admire her. But when the tears came into her eyes, and she could not find the words to thank him, he thought perhaps he had made a mistake to give her violets A couple of heartless orchids would have been better. Violets are too nostalgic.

On the embankment, where the lights gleamed on the dark water, they stopped again and he got out and lifted his hat to say goodbye, but she said, "I will get out for a moment. It is so cool and fresh here." They walked a few paces together and then stopped, and though London roared behind them it seemed strangely quiet. In the quiet they heard clocks striking and the voice of the river flowing by; and Colonel Anstruther thought he heard again the running footsteps of the rescuing Child. Then Mrs. Rodney asked, scarcely above her breath, "Is is true?"

He knew what was in her mind and turning to her he answered gently, "I believe so. I believe there is a mystery burning like a light behind the appearance of things. Or you could say it is a peace at the heart of our tumult. On such a day as this moments of quiet take us by surprise. Have you not found it so?"

She said, "Can dreams of the happy past be more than memory?"

He answered, "Why not? There is no time in dreams. They can just as well be indications of the future."

They walked back to the car and when he had thanked her and said goodbye he stood waiting, hat in hand, for her to get in. With her foot on the step she turned back to him and said shyly, "I do not like to say goodbye. Can you lunch with me one day?"

He had finished with such social occasions, he had thought and hoped, but he realized suddenly, with grateful humility, that the power of succour was not yet dead in him. Knowing this he could do no other than thank her and give her his card, with the address of his club upon it. Then he stepped back and she got in and the car glided on. Looking back at him she saw that he was a very old man, older than she had thought, but she knew with a sense of strength and comfort that his wisdom would be all the greater for her need.

Saint Nicolas

Saint Nicolas

I

IT WAS CHRISTMAS EVE, in a century long ago, and the old country town had robed itself in magic. The first snow had fallen, a light fall but enough to powder the steep gabled roofs and cobbled streets with virgin whiteness. The frost fires sparkled upon it, and overhead the stars were a weight of glory in the sky. From sheer goodwill doors had been left ajar and windows uncurtained, so that bright beams of light lay across the snow. Festive smells floated out from the doors, scents of baked meats and roasting apples, ale and wine, spices and perfumes, and the fragrant smoke of innumerable fires of apple wood and beech logs and resinous pine branches. The bells rang out and all the children of the town seemed laughing. They were glad it was a fine evening, for the Players had come. Their stage was set up even now in the yard of the White Hart Inn, and decorated with lanterns and mistletoe and great boughs of fir and yew and holly. In another hour the trumpet would sound, and all the people would come streaming into the inn yard, and up the steps to the galleries, packing themselves into every inch of space, and then the pealing of the trumpet would come again, and then upon that stage that seemed set up at the heart of the world the

E

Players would show forth once again the story of Christ's birth.

How dared they do it? wondered the actor who played the devil, as he sat repairing his tail in the disused inn stable where the Players would live and sleep and eat until they took to the road again. The stable was too derelict to be used any longer for the horses of the quality, but the Players were used to discomfort, and it opened on the yard just behind their stage and so was convenient for them. And no doubt, thought Old Nick, it was a lot more comfortable than the one where Christ was born.

"Lord have mercy on us!" he murmured. "Such a set of scoundrels as we are."

He always felt this shame when the time came round to play again the story of Christ's birth. Such a good-for-nothing lot, as men, and as actors not much better. Yet each year he hoped that this time, just this once, they would give a perfect performance. But of course they never did, least of all himself. Not that it mattered about him, for he was only the devil. Perhaps this year, just this last time——

He caught himself up. Why did he keep thinking that this year, for him, it was the last time? Master Roper, of course, had only yesterday threatened to kick him out for reasons of age, infirmity and general incompetence, but then he had been doing that for the last five years. In reality he found Old Nick uncommonly useful. Ugly as the poor old devil was, and full of eccentricities, he was the butt of the company and kept them all good humoured. He was good with the children, and any who had fallen sick. And he was a useful scapegoat. Master Roper was accustomed to visit the sins of the whole lot of them upon Old Nick, for it drove them mad to have the old devil kicked and abused, and he kept the whip hand of them that way. Proud man though he was Old Nick did not mind because he was glad to be of use. Especially to the children.

Laying down his mended tail he looked at the two little boys where they lay beside him, asleep on a pile of hay, warmly covered by the Lady's cloak. It would break his heart to part from the children. What would they do without him? He was father and mother to them both. He pushed the thought aside and reached for Gabriel's robe, that needed a patch behind. He had learned to sew after a fashion. Indeed he had had to learn to do most things after a fashion because he was always too proud to ask for help, and such people must do everything for themselves or perish. He very nearly had perished, time and again, because he was not very bright and did things only after a fashion and never very well. He had been born a failure and as life went on had sunk always a little lower, but he had never accepted charity on that account. Nor sympathy either. 'Proud as the devil.' He'd always been proud, and they said it was a sin.

"God be merciful to me a sinner," he prayed. He knew he needed mercy for he was getting old and, so far as he could see, was for all his striving no nearer heaven than when he started out. The fact was, he thought gloomily, he only followed his Lord after a fashion.

2

TO CHEER HIMSELF up he looked again at the cloak. It was made of warm black cloth and lined with lambswool, and the Lady had pulled it off her own shoulders to give to the children. It had been only three days ago and he remembered the scene as vividly as though he were re-living it.

Her coach had come round the corner of the narrow lane rather unexpectedly, and somehow the Players' poor old cart, piled high with stage properties and costumes and the children, got upset into the ditch; Old Nick was driving it and he only drove after a fashion. Although her coachman was in no way to blame the Lady stopped the coach and got out, and made her serving man help the Players pull the boxes and bags out of the ditch, and haul out the cart and bony horse. Old Nick, as soon as he had scrambled out himself, got the children out, and then oblivious of everyone else sat down on a big boulder at the side of the lane to comfort them. He took the little golden-haired Tom Thumb on his knee and blew his nose, and then he opened his pack and dived into it for a bit of gingerbread to comfort Benjie. Tom Thumb did not care for gingerbread. He liked hot bread and milk but he did not get it very often. Knowing he wasn't going to get it now he burrowed into the crook of Old Nick's arm and tried to get warm that way. Benjie, a dark-haired, grave-faced little boy, was past the burrowing age, but he leaned against Old Nick's knee on the other side and looked up at the Lady out of his great dark sad eyes as he munched his gingerbread. Absorbed in the children Old Nick did not even know the Lady was there until she spoke to him.

"Are they your own children, good Sir?"

He looked up then and saw her, and with Tom Thumb still in the crook of his arm got up and bowed to her.

"No, Lady. I have no children."

The cold wind blew keenly down the lane and the sky was heavy with unshed snow. The whole world was grey and desolate and the Lady shivered and drew her cloak more closely about her. Old Nick did not permit himself to shiver. He stood straight and tall and gaunt and his scarecrow garments flapped about him in the wind. She thought she had never seen an uglier man. His sallow face was pock-marked and his dark eyebrows had an upward tilt at the corners such as one sees in pictures of the devil. His eyes squinted to such an extent that she did not think that either of them were looking at her, until an amused quirk at the corners of his mouth told her that he knew quite well what she was thinking. There was a kindly mockery in his face now, and pride in his stiff figure. From habit her hand had moved towards the purse in her pocket, but now she quickly withdrew it and did not insult him with her pity. But in her heart she offered him her sympathy, even as he was offering his to her. She too was childless and she was always glad when Christmas was over; yes, glad, even though it was that season when the thought of the Child in the manger broke hard hearts and bent stiff wills, and queer flowers of understanding bloomed and flourished in unexpected places, and between unlikely people; as now on a wind-swept road between a proud great Lady and a proud poor man who had never seen each other before and had nothing in common except their pride, the children and the Child.

For they both worshipped the Child, and the children in Him and for Him. Suddenly they knew that of each other.

She swept the cloak off her shoulders and gave it to him. "For the children," she said. "To keep them warm. For His sake."

He bowed and smiled, and took it and did not mind at all, for there was suddenly no pride left in him. And she got into her coach and drove away, and though she had no cloak now, and knew her servants mocked at her, she did not mind, because there was for the moment no pride left in her either.

3

HE THOUGHT MUCH of her as he sat patching Gabriel's robe. He had these two adopted waifs to care for, the child actors of the company, but he pictured her living in some great house, widowed and barren and no longer young, and perhaps now unloving and unloved by human kind. If that was the case he was the wealthier of the two, for really all the Players were his children, not only Tom Thumb and Benjie.

He kept an anxious eye on the stable door as he sewed, for very soon now they would be coming in to dress for the play and to-night of all nights he was desperately anxious that they should be in good shape . . . To play the story of Christ's birth . . . It would, he thought, be ridiculous presumption for even the best of men to attempt to set forth such great matters, but when it came to a rapscallion company of vagabond good-for-nothings—he pulled himself up sharply. It was for good-for-nothings that Christ had died. And at least he and Herod were God-fearing men who could be relied upon to keep sober. He pulled himself up again, for there were worse sins than a mug of ale too much now and again. Pride, for instance. And in any case, in his experience, it was always the same in the theatrical profession. Your noble blue-eyed hero was always a proper scoundrel and your villain an honest fellow on the whole.

The stable door was flung open and Gabriel came in on a gust of wind. His battered cap with its peacock's feather was clapped on the side of his curly red head at a riotous angle, and the condition of his torn cherry-coloured doublet suggested that during the course of an argument someone had flung a bucket of pigwash at him. But he looked cheerful, his rosy cheeks distended by the apple he was munching, and his gait was only slightly unsteady. He'd be all right, Old Nick decided thankfully, after he'd stuck his flaming head in a bucket of cold water. And so would the two young shepherds, who came in a few moments after; merry, but not more so than boys should be at Christmas time. Poor old Kit, the old shepherd, could always be relied on to keep out of mischief because he was too decrepit to do anything else. He'd not been out like the young fellows. He had spent the day huddled up by the little fire of glowing coals that Old Nick had lit for him in the brazier, trying to keep warm. That was four of them safe. Herod was not here yet, but he, good humble selfless fellow, never let anyone down. Saint Joseph could be relied on too, though at the thought of him Old Nick's face tightened grimly. For Master Roper himself played Joseph, the great benign beard he put on for the occasion a most admirable disguise, and it was a torment to Old Nick that such a whited sepulchre should play the part of the foster-father of the Lord. It was almost impossible to remember that for him too the Lord had died.

But where was Mary? There were no women in the company and Will, who played Mary, was a perpetual anxiety. He was on the whole a good boy, and certainly a beautiful boy, with his clear treble voice that remained so long unbroken, his mild dark eyes and pale oval face, but he was an inveterate and indomitable fighter. His fragile appearance was entirely deceptive, and so was the mildness of his eyes. He would go on fighting until he was beaten to a jelly; and still he would go on fighting. The gutters of every town they played in ran with his blood, but it would boil up again by the time they reached the next one. Old Nick took great care of Will, giving him most of his own food to build up his anaemic condition and sitting up with him night after night putting goose-grease on his bruises. And Will loved Old Nick and had promised not to go out to-night . . . Yet he was not here.

The Magi came in, and Herod and the Trumpeter, and the Innkeeper, but still no Mary.

With a sense of disaster growing upon him Old Nick woke up Benjie and Tom Thumb and dressed them. They were the cherubs who worshipped at the crib and they wore white tunics, small gold halos and little feather wings. Old Nick had these heavenly garments in his special care and kept them as clean as he could; though not as clean as he could wish because he only laundered after a fashion. In his care, too, was the crude little figure that he had carved from a bit of wood (he carved only after a fashion) and wrapped in swaddling bands. He kept it in a box by the children's bed and felt for it such reverence that his feeling had communicated itself to the rest of the Players, good-for-nothings though they were. The corner of the various outhouses where the children slept, and where the Babe lay, seemed to them always a place apart. Old Nick was mostly to be found there too and so it was also their refuge in all times of trouble, perplexity or downright disaster.

The stable door opened again and to the corner where Old Nick was washing the children's faces Will came stumbling in his tribulation. He was speechless because his upper lip had been badly cut, and it was a wonder he had been able to see his way to the corner, because both his eyes were closed up. His nose was bleeding and he was shaking as though he had the ague. But it was not because of his physical misfortunes that he was so miserable. It was because he had broken his promise. He would not be able to play Mary. And his sins would be visited by Master Roper not upon him but upon Old Nick. Will could not speak or look his penitence but he stood before Old Nick with his head hanging, and when there was no word of reproach he began to sob.

Old Nick took the boy in his arms and laid him down on the straw where the children had been sleeping, and washed his face and covered him up with the Lady's cloak. Then he turned and looked bleakly at the rest of the company, who had gathered round in consternation. Not a single one of them could play Mary. Gabriel must play Gabriel. Of the two young shepherds one was round and fat and the other was wizened and hunchbacked, and the voices of both of them had already broken.

"Look after Will," Old Nick said to the others. "Now then, Tom Thumb, don't cry. I'll go and tell Master Roper."

4

HE WENT OUTSIDE, where the stage was waiting, garlanded and gay with the lighted lanterns swinging at the four corners. The audience was already streaming in, happy and laughing in their bright clothes, gathering about the stage and climbing up the stairs to the outside galleries. Light streamed out from the inn and overhead the stars were sparkling. Master Roper always had his own room at the inns and never shared the draughty barns and stables that housed his Players, and Old Nick turned into the panelled hall of the White Hart to ask where he might find him. It was a good inn, that sometimes housed the quality, and coming down the stairs, wearing now a blue cloak and holding up her sweeping blue gown, was the Lady. When she saw Old Nick she smiled without surprise, as though he were an old friend whom she had expected to see there.

"Saint Nicolas, how are the children?" she asked. And then she went on companionably, "A wheel has come off my coach and I am waiting here in the warm while they put it on again . . . Saint Nicolas, are you in any trouble?"

As companionably as she had told him about the coach wheel he told her about Will. She stood thinking for a moment, and then she asked, "Could I play Mary? It would not take you long, would it, to tell me what I must do?"

"But, Lady, your reputation!" he gasped.

"I do not live in the town," she said, "and I do not think there would be anyone who would recognise me." Then she lifted her head proudly. "Nor should I mind if they did."

He looked at her. She had a slender figure and a clear treble voice. The blue veil over her head would hide her greying hair. She might very well pass for a boy and she would play the part with grace.

"Thank you, Lady," he said. "I had wanted this performance to be very perfect."

At the stable door, standing beside him as he fumbled for the latch, she said, "I hope I shall not fail you. I know by heart all the words that Mary speaks. Sometimes I have felt that I understood her a little." She paused, as though she had a little difficulty in breathing. "I had a son once, but they killed him in the Wars."

He could think of nothing to say, and so said nothing, but he was grateful for the honour done him.

It was, as Old Nick had hoped it would be, a perfect performance. The presence of the Lady, moving among them with such a loving dignity, as though she were the mother of them all, drew from each actor the best that he had to give. Even Master Roper gave of his best, and reserved what he had to say about the events of the evening until the performance should be safely over. Old Nick had not to appear until the end, when he would leap upon the stage with a flash and a bang to fetch Herod away to where he belonged, and hidden among the greenery he watched spellbound. How could he ever have thought of this woman as barren? She might have borne one son only, and he taken from her and killed while still in his young manhood, but once a mother always a

mother, through life and death and through eternity. She seemed
to him not only the Mother of the figures who moved about her
on the stage but the Mother of the entranced audience of men and
women and children who packed the courtyard, the stairs and
galleries, the Mother of the whole world, the Mother of heaven,
the Mother of God. Mary had borne only the one Son, the Child
she held in her arms, but he held in his love all that was, heaven
and earth, angels and archangels, men and women and children,
because he had made them and was their God, and so she, holding
him, held them too. The hushed audience worshipped him by
their reverent silence, the actors, those good-for-nothings, worshipped him by their movements, and his Mother worshipped
him as she sat there with him in her arms, on the stage that is set
up on Christmas Eve at the heart of the world.

5

IN THIS LIFE one can fall very quickly from heaven to a sort of hell,
and Old Nick was scarcely aware of any passage of time between
the sounding of the trumpet that told the audience the play was
finished and the moment he came back from seeing the Lady to
her coach, and found Master Roper in the stable most cruelly
belabouring Will before the horrified eyes of all the players.
Hitherto, except for a few kicks here and there, Master Roper
had not been accustomed to use physical violence upon the boys;
he had chosen the more subtle method of visiting their delin-
quencies upon Old Nick, which hurt them infinitely more. But
now something or other, perhaps the fall from the heights to
which he had attained on the stage to what he was, the realisation
of the contrast between Saint Joseph and Will Roper, had driven
him quite mad. He had pulled poor Will to his feet and was
beating him about the head, so that his nose had started to bleed
again and the cuts on his face reopened. And the Players, so
recently in heaven, were all too shocked and sickened to do anything at all about it.

And for a moment Old Nick could do nothing either, until he
saw the children, still in their angels' wings and halos, Benjie
clasping the wooden Babe in his arms, looking on with great

wondering eyes of astonishment. Master Roper's great hand, swinging back for a fresh blow, caught Tom Thumb on the side of his golden head, and he fell headlong with tears and lamentations. That sent Old Nick mad too. With all the force that still remained in his spent old body he hit Master Roper a crack on the jaw that sent him staggering. Then he picked up the almost unconscious Will and laid him back on the straw beneath the Lady's cloak, grabbed Benjie and the wooden Babe under one arm and Tom Thumb under the other, shouted to Herod to open the stable door, and vanished like a flash of lightning.

Would she be gone? No, the coach was moving only very slowly along the street over the ruts of frozen snow. Gasping and staggering he caught up with it and shouted to the coachman to stop. Then he wrenched open the door and flung the children inside.

"Take them!" he cried to her.

"Why?" she asked. "What has happened?" But even while she spoke her arms, holding the folds of her cloak, lifted like wings and the children were gathered in. Then her arms fell and there was nothing to be seen of them except the top of Tom Thumb's golden head where she held him in the crook of her arm.

Still gasping for breath Old Nick told her as well as he could. "Take them and keep them," he commanded her. "Do you want them to grow up grey-faced and wizened like the hunchback boy? Or drunken and dissolute while still in their teens like the boy who played Gabriel? Or to lie in their blood on a stable floor like Will? Or to be as I am? Take them and keep them, and the Child too, for Christ's Sake." And he banged the coach door, turned away and left her.

"Stop!" she cried. "Stop! Come back!"

She knew by the proud way that his head jerked up that he had heard her, but he did not stop and he did not come back. She would have saved him, if she could, from what lay before him now. She was weeping as the coach drove on. Yet in his place she would have done the same. She would have preferred to die forsaken in a ditch than live the pensioner of a rich woman. She, too, had often been described as "proud as the devil."

The fate she had envisaged for him fell upon Old Nick almost immediately. Kicked out at last by Master Roper, Christmas Day found him tramping along the road a homeless vagabond. He did not mind much, for it was what he had always expected. Failure that he was, doing things only after a fashion and sinking as life went on always a little lower, he had known he would come to this. Death was always a difficult act of penance, he thought, and to die of hunger and exhaustion in a snowy ditch was no worse an end than many a rich man had to face. He missed the children, of course, but on this day, of all days in the year, he had the Child, and the glow of possession warmed him through. Nevertheless as he toiled along he murmured often, "God be merciful to me, a sinner," for he was tramping now to the end of the way and, as far as he could see, was for all his striving no nearer heaven than when he started out.

John

John

IT STRUCK HIM suddenly that it was odd to be bothering to sweep the floor when the world had come to an end and love was dead. What was the use? And by the light of a candle too. One could not see to sweep properly by the light of a candle. But there had to be a candle because it was night. The light of the world had been put out and it was night. He stopped and looked down for a moment, in the dim light, at the broom handle and his thin brown hands tautly holding it, clutching at it in a stupid desperate sort of way as though it were a spar of wood that kept him from drowning. Well, so it was. The everyday tasks, chopping the wood, carrying the water from the well, washing the dishes, sweeping the floor, did keep one from drowning in grief, going mad from the shock of what one had seen, what one remembered, what one had done.

What one had *done*. That was the worst of it. He had run away. They had all run away. If they hadn't it might not have happened. Not that he was concerned with what the others had done, it was his own running away that was the weak trembling of his limbs, the tight band of pain jammed down over his temples, the stabbing through his hands and feet, the appalling knowledge in his mind that his pain was only the feeblest echo of the pain he had seen. And yet his friend, who had borne it, had never run away.

Courage forsaken by cowardice, truth betrayed by lies, love tortured by hatred, life put out by death. And then darkness and the ending of the world. He had run away. He'd come back, of course, but it had been too late then. Nothing to be done then but stand there through the endless hours and watch it happen, the sight searing through his brain and the agony of his helplessness choking him. Too late then. It had taken him exactly two minutes to run away but the agony of his friend had gone on for hours. If he could only have back that two minutes and do it again, do it differently. But he couldn't. It was too late. And love was dead. In spite of a confused feeling of unbelief he knew that must be true because for a moment or two, while Joseph smoothed out the winding sheet, he had held love, dead, in his arms. Dead because he had run away. Lord God, help me, he prayed, I'll go mad if I go on like this; like those poor devils who used to fall screaming at the Master's feet, and he'd put out his hands and hold them steady. But there was no one, now, to hold him steady, to hold any poor wretch steady. He'd seen to that by running away.

Stop it, you fool! Stop thinking! He began to sweep the floor again and the dust went round and round in whirls. He couldn't seem to get the dust where he wanted it. He was a complete fool. When he'd carried in water from the well last night he'd only stumbled over the door step and upset the bucket. And Mary, his Mother too now, had mopped up the water and comforted him. In greater grief than any of them yet it was she who was their strength. But then she had not run away. She only, of them all, was guiltless in the darkness of this night. She had the strength of her sinlessness, and of some memory to which she clung; something her son had said about 'the third day'. There was a vague memory of that in John's mind too, it was the source of that feeling he had that death could not be true, but his confused mind could not seem to get hold of it.

What was happening? The candle flame dipped and swayed, the floor seemed slipping away beneath him and there was a rumble like thunder. Only another earthquake shock. He steadied himself. Usually earthquakes terrified him, only nothing mattered now. But he hoped the women would be safe, going through the dark streets to the garden. But there was no further shock. That was all; except that the atmosphere seemed curiously freshened, as though a clean wind blew down the world. Yet there was no wind. There was something, though. He blinked his sleepless red-rimmed eyes and looked about him. What was it? Light! The endless night was over and the first light of dawn was slowly filling the little room, flowing into it like water through the small square window. The light lapped about his body, that ached with such an intolerable weariness. It seemed to rise about him, taking away the pain. It was a brightness about the broom handle and it touched his hands.

He felt that it held his hands. He had always been a highly-strung restless sort of creature and when he was nervous and excited his hands would shake. Sometimes the Master had put His own hand over them, holding them still. Not often, because the Master had never been very free with his caresses, his love not being of that type; the grasp of the hand, the word of endearment, were given when they were necessary but not when they were not. Yet now, as the light rose and strengthened, he distinctly felt the grasp of a living hand. He knew the feel of that hand so well; wide across the palm because accustomed to the handling of an oar, hardened by the tools of His trade, the fingers very strong and supple. Yet the hardness and the strength had given a reassurance more comforting than any softness and the warmth of the hand had always sent a glow of courage right through one's body. He felt that glow now. It rose with the light and reached his heart, that had been thumping so oddly. It reached his sore eyes and aching temples. Just his fancy, of course, about the touch, for the Master was dead, but straightening himself he found that day had come. And his splitting headache had gone. The broom was not so heavy now and there was strength in his body. He got the dust where he wanted it, opened the door and swept it out of doors.

He knocked the broom handle against the side of the door, and then paused, for it was such an extraordinarily lovely dawn. It struck him as odd that he should be able to notice the loveliness, but he did. It was still very early, yet the pearly light held already some faint rumour of the coming glory of the sunrise. It held colours soft and delicate as the colours of a reflected rainbow, incredibly gentle yet pervasive, as though the world in sleep had soaked up mercy like the air we breathe. Why did the word mercy come to his mind? There had been no mercy in the world two days

F

ago. Mercy, with love, had died. Yet today, in this dawn, it was alive again.

There was still that freshness in the air. He took great gulps of it as though it were cool water from a well. He leaned against the door and the blessed coolness of it seemed gently to close his eyes. It was incredible relief to keep his eyes shut for a little while. He had scarcely been able to close them the last two nights because of what he saw when the lids came down. He had not known before that memory could paint such pictures upon closed lids. Perhaps that was one of the things that drove men mad—looking at the pictures they saw when they closed their eyes—things they'd seen, things they'd done. Perhaps that was what was torturing Peter, for he'd lain all night with closed lids, yet not sleeping. But no, it wouldn't be what he saw that he could hardly bear, for he hadn't been there, it would be what he heard. His own voice speaking. Three times over he'd said it. At the first cockcrow this morning a rigor like the rigor of death had seemed to take his body. John, lying beside him on his mat, had got up and come downstairs to sweep the floor, for he had known that the only thing he could do for the man at that moment was to leave him alone.

He wished Peter could hear what he was hearing now— the singing of birds. They were waking in the gardens of Jerusalem and their liquid notes were cool as the air and beautiful as the new-born light. Were they singing like this in the garden where love was laid in the tomb, the garden where the women were? The women had left the house very early, while it was yet dark, with the spices for the embalming. There had not been time for that on that fearful Friday night. They had not been able to do more than wrap their dead Master in his grave clothes . . . Dead . . . But the word that in spite of his queer unbelief had been stabbing him like a spear in his side for so many hours no longer stabbed him. It was as though the wound had healed, as though the world itself was dead. He opened his eyes and saw the whole of the sky covered with small crisp rosy clouds like feathers, with behind them an incredible depth of blue. And the scent of flowers came on the wind.

It was then that he heard the running feet, coming so quickly and lightly, yet with such a desperate urgency. He stood braced now, one hand pressed against the door, his heart beating in sickening thuds. For he knew even before he saw her who it was who was running down the street. Only Mary of Magdala had such fleetness of foot, only she could put such a note of eager desperation into all she did and was.

She was with him in a moment, clinging to him like a child, the veil fallen back from her bright head, and like a child she was crying and gasping and talking all at once so that he could make out nothing of what she was trying to tell him. Her clamour hurt him. It hurt the stillness and peace of the heavenly dawn. He pulled her inside the house and shut the door.

"Mary be quiet! Don't cry like that. What's the good? And I can't understand."

But he held her gently, for he was gentle by nature, and grief had so completely locked them all together through these dreadful days that all of them who loved their Master seemed now one body. And then the passionate simplicity of Mary's childlike nature always called forth protectiveness. She poured her whole being into the joy or despair of the moment so that like a child she must be held in safety till the storm was past.

"They have taken him away! They have taken him away! He's not there!" she gasped.

"Who have taken him away? What are you talking about?"

"The robbers. He's gone. John! John! Robbers have stolen the Master."

"No, that's not possible. They sealed the stone and set a guard."

It was not John who had spoken now but Peter. He had heard her crying and had come to them, and though he was in greater misery than John he was at the moment more clear-headed. For him the impossible thing had happened and the unbearable thing was being borne. He knew his Master had died. He knew it better than John did, who had seen him die. There is a sense in which it is easier to know a thing if you have not seen it. John's mind these last two nights had beaten this way and that in confusion among the unbelievable things he had seen, so that he had become exhausted by unbelief, but his had lain still with the impossible in cold agony until at last he knew it true. And the truth about himself he knew too. The loyal courageous hero of his daydreams, the man whose love would never deny or forsake how-ever hard the test, did not exist at all. He was a man without courage, without loyalty, without truth and without love. For two nights he had lain with the unbearable knowledge but at the sound of Mary's crying he had got up, bearing it, and gone to see what he could do. Such acceptance had made him very clear-headed but it had also aged him. The sight of his face, when she raised her head and looked at him over John's shoulder, stilled Mary's lamentations as John's gentle endearments had not been able to do. She had not known before that a man could become old so quickly as this.

"Sit down, Mary," said Peter quietly. He took her from John's arms and sat her down on the stool. He stood by her and awkwardly stroked the braids of her hair. For the moment she was quieted and said sensibly, "The stone has been rolled away and the guard has gone. They fled in a panic. You can see they did because there's a lantern overturned and a couple of spears left behind. And the grass and the flowers are trampled where they ran. It was grave robbers. You can see it was." And then the horror of it came over her again and she jumped up, twisted herself free from John's detaining hand and ran for the door. She collided there with Salome, John's mother, and Mary Cleopas, but she pushed them away and ran out into the street and away again like the wind. It seemed to her bruised mind that if she went back to the garden again perhaps she would find him.

"Mary!" cried Salome. "Come back!"

"Let her alone," said Peter heavily. "Is it true, Salome?"

Both the older women, breathless and panting, for they too had run through the streets, began to talk at once. Until now they had been calmer than Mary, for they had lived longer in this world and had known the death of many hopes and stood by many graves, but now they were nearly as incoherent as she had been. But with joy, not despair. For the tomb was not empty, they said. There were two men there. Sun-lit, they seemed. Yes, sun-lit in that dark place. They sat one at the head and one at the foot where the body of Jesus had lain, and they said the Lord was risen. Not stolen, but risen. Mary, poor girl, had not seemed to see anything. She had not waited to hear and see. She had never had much patience, poor Mary, and without patience there is neither hope nor faith nor vision. But they had heard and seen. Not seen, exactly, for they had not been able to look on those shining faces. Nor heard, really; not like you hear men speaking

in the ordinary way. Yet they *had* heard; like you hear news that
shakes you in the song of a bird, a shepherd's pipe calling in the
hills, a child singing at the well; you hear and you set down your
pitcher and the tears are on your face. But they knew what they
had to say. They had to come quickly and say, he is alive, he is
risen, "Lo, I have told you."

The bird told you, the shepherd's pipe, the child singing at the
well, the sun-lit man who had looked down at the slab of holy
stone and then passed his hand across his shining eyes. They said
the same thing.

Afterwards John could hardly disentangle the women's confused
words from the thoughts that had lit into flame in his own mind.
Nor did he remember how he had got himself out into the street,
away from the women's talk, and from Peter's sad eyes that
looked pitifully upon them and thought they talked the nonsense
of silly women who have borne too much. There seemed wings on
his feet for a while, and then he heard Peter calling after him and
slackened speed that the older man might catch up. They ran for a
little side by side but they could not speak; Peter because he was
panting with the exhaustion of John's speed, John because of the
tumultuous hope that was in him. Now and then he looked at
Peter, but the man's rugged furrowed face was still set in the lines
of his stony grief. He ran so doggedly and so desperately because
he thought they might yet catch the robbers. But he could not
stay the course. The sweat started out on his forehead and he
gasped and stumbled as the pain caught his side. John ran on and
came first to the tomb.

But he could not go in. His nature, fine-drawn and sensitive,
was not disciplined enough as yet to have attained to that perfect
poise he had so worshipped in his Master. His own will was still
beloved by him. His Master, though far more highly strung,
more intensely sensitive than he, had been held in perfect balance
by the iron strength of His devotion to the will of God. But John
swung this way and that, intensely happy when things went as he
wanted them to go, miserable when they did not, now courageous,
now afraid. When he was with his Master he had felt like a small
boat, swinging with the tides, yet safely moored to a great
strength; he would not be swept to disaster, either one way or the
other, while the rope held. But two days ago it had seemed to
break and there had seemed no bottom to the misery into which

he had fallen. But there had been a bottom, because there had come that unbelief in the fact of death, the peace of the fair dawn, his winged feet, his hope that as the misery had only seemed to be bottomless so the rope had only seemed to break. But now—he could not go in. His frail boat had swung the other way. If he were to go in now and see no shining ones, see only the empty slab of cold and cruel stone, or worse still a heap of tumbled grave-clothes flung there by thieves, then it would kill him. It would be the last thing he could not bear. He leaned against the rock, panting from his run, his heart thudding, his head buried in the crook of his arm, and the pictures began again in his mind, not this time pictures of what he had seen but of what he might have seen if he had watched the thieves in the tomb. Peter came up to him, paused a moment, and then with something of his old impetuosity went on into the tomb. But John could not follow him. If he went in he would see the tumbled grave-clothes.

But he had courage and it returned to him as the thudding of his heart quieted. He must go in. He must know one way or the other. And he could not leave Peter alone in there. Moving gallantly now, with the grace of his youth, he bent his comely head and went in. He saw no heavenly spirits and the light was dim. He saw Peter on his knees staring stupidly at the slab of rock where the Master had lain. And then he saw what he had dreaded to see, the grave-clothes left behind, and it was in truth as though he died. He could not groan or cry out. He was too cold. He just stood there, gripped by the cold. This was death—this cold. To have had the glorious hope, and lost it. To be forsaken of hope. To be forsaken in this cold. Was this what the Master had felt when in the dark garden they had forsaken him and fled? His mind, that had been so hot and confused, was suddenly coldly clear, as Peter's had been. He and Peter had changed places now, for looking at Peter's face he saw only bewilderment there, not a full comprehension of the fearful thing that had happened. He looked back again at the grave-clothes and the whole terrible clarity of his mind became focused upon them.

They were not in a tumbled heap. They lay in dignity, every fold in place. No human hands had touched them since the hands of the Marys had so disposed those folds. And the small bunches of herbs that the women had placed here and there among the folds were still where they had put them. Only as there was no body within the grave-clothes they had sunk gently to the stone by their own weight, just as a lily flower might fall softly to the ground below, still keeping its perfect shape. The shape of the grave-clothes was very perfect. Naturally, thought John, for the shape of the body that had been withdrawn had been perfect. And the shape of his head too. The napkin, lying apart by itself, kept the shape of the head. No one had disturbed it. God had taken to himself his human body once again with supreme gentleness as well as supreme power. But the gentleness and the power had for John a most dear familiarity.

Without knowing what he did he fell on his knees too. He wondered why he had thought the tomb so dark, for the light of the sun filled it. He saw no heavenly spirits; for him they were not necessary. He heard no voice speaking, but he heard the birds singing outside in the garden. Was the Master outside in the garden? Mary, perhaps, had seen him. Yet John stayed where he was, for he who had forsaken his Lord did not deserve to see his Lord. But he knew that he would see him again; if not in this life then in another, because the gentleness and the power were but different aspects of eternal mercy. John could wait. Length of time no longer mattered. Nothing mattered but the fact of Life.

Giovanni

Giovanni

No one but the holy man up on the hill could do anything with Giovanni. He was wild as a leveret and mischievous as a jackdaw, but because he was an attractive small boy quite a number of the kindly people in the Vale of Rietti would have been glad to give him a more permanent home than the temporary shelter he would occasionally accept, if the weather was bad or his stomach empty. Besides, it gave the valley a bad name to have an orphan boy running around apparently uncared for and unloved. But Giovanni did not wish to be cared for, and as for love, he had the birds and animals and the holy man whom men called Brother Francis, and these two loves satisfied his heart. He loved the creatures because they were wild as himself and he loved Brother Francis because he shared his tastes, disliking a roof over his head except in winter, and only then because the fire on the hearth was bright and gay to look at, and loving the sun and moon and stars as though they were his friends. He also liked to sing, and so did Giovanni. Brother Francis would pick up two sticks and pretend they were a viol and a bow, and he would pass the bow across the imaginary strings and he and Giovanni would sing together to the accompaniment that both of them heard very clearly. Brother Francis was always gay with Giovanni and the little boy was sorry that he did not live always in the hermitage on the slope of Monte

Rainerio, but only came occasionally to rest and pray. Giovanni always knew when he was there. He knew it as the birds know when food has been put out for them. That is, he knew.

He knew it now. Indeed he had known it in the middle of last night, when he had felt the rain coming through the straw roof of the deserted shepherd's hut where he had curled up to sleep, and his heart had jumped for joy because his friend was here. But he was sorry about the weather because rain seemed all wrong when Brother Francis was there. He loved light, and loved it so much that when Giovanni had asked him once what God was like he had said he was like light. He had said that the glorious sun in the sky is like God the Father, and the sunshine coming down from the sun and warming us through and through is like Christ our Saviour, and that both of them dwell within the hearts of all men as a gift of light that is God the Holy Spirit. Giovanni had taken this quite literally and when his heart jumped for joy he would see with his inside eyes the leap of a bright flame. And when it had jumped it would die down again and he would see a round, glowing ball lying still like a coal in the fire. This ball would glow with love, or anger or pity, but it only jumped when Giovanni was suddenly happy. But his outside eyes could not see it, and this grieved him, so that at present he preferred the sun and the light of the sun, and he was sorry it was raining.

At the first gleam of a grey dawn he was up and away and scrambling up through the wet woods towards the hermitage. He knew every twist and turn of the rough path and soon saw up above him the caves in the rock that formed the hermitage, and the small stone chapel that Brother Francis had built with his own hands and dedicated to Santa Maria Maddalena. He moved with caution now for Brother Francis did not always come alone to Monte Rainerio, sometimes he brought one or two of the brothers with him, and though they were fond of Giovanni, and had told him with laughter that he was one of them because he ran barefoot about the world, they did sometimes shoo away visitors if Brother Francis was at prayer. Giovanni did not tell on them, though he knew Brother Francis did not like people to be shooed away, because one does not tell on one's brothers, however objectionable they may be.

But the coast seemed clear and he came quietly to the chapel, where Brother Francis was usually to be found in the early mornings. He was there now. Standing in the doorway Giovanni could see him kneeling before the rough stone altar with his face buried in his hands, and he was weeping. Never having seen his friend anything but merry Giovanni was shocked and scared, and with that live coal inside his heart burning with pity he forgot about not interrupting Brother Francis at his prayers and ran to him, kneeling down beside him and tugging at the cord that bound his brown habit about his waist. "What's the matter, Brother Francis?" he demanded. "Have you toothache?"

Brother Francis looked down at the child kneeling beside him. "My son," he said, "I should have preferred toothache to this grief."

"What grief?" demanded Giovanni.

It was typical of Francis of Assissi that he should answer the child's question with the truth. Child-like at heart he did not distinguish very clearly between boys and grown men. They were all his children.

"There are many of my sons who are tired of going barefoot about the world," he said. "They wish me to change the rules of our Order, that they may have less hardship. They are weary of following the example of Our Lord Jesus Christ. I cannot see my way. The light has gone out within me."

A shadow fell upon them. Giovanni looked up and saw that one of the brothers had come in, a man he did not know. He was shivering and oppressed with gloom and raindrops were dripping off the point of his thin nose. He was also extremely angry at finding a wet grubby boy interrupting Brother Francis at his prayers, and he would have boxed the boy's ears had not Giovanni dived under his arm and run away down into the wood, despite Brother Francis's cry to him that he should come back. He wasn't going to come back to have his ears boxed, for he had his dignity to consider. But he bore no ill will against the shivering brother. He must be a new one for the old ones whom he knew, Leo and Juniper and the others, had learnt to control their shivers long ago. It must be the new ones who were tired of following the example of Our Lord Jesus Christ, and in weather like this one could understand how they felt.

All that wet day Giovanni was wondering what he could do to comfort Brother Francis because the light in his heart had gone out. But when he went to sleep that night he had'nt thought of anything, and when he woke up in the morning he still hadn't thought. But the rain had passed in the night and the sun was shining so he forgot his sorrow, leaped up in joy and ran out of the hut.

The sun had not risen very far. It shone in glory just above the trees at the end of the meadow and the whole world was brimming with its light. Giovanni danced up and down in the light and the light warmed him. And then he saw the most wonderful thing. The whole meadow, stretching from his feet to the sun, was sparkling as though it were on fire, as though every wet flower and blade of grass was carrying a tongue of flame. The light was so brilliant that it dazzled the eyes. Blinking, Giovanni bent down and picked a small blue flower with rayed petals that grew at his feet. He looked at it and saw that it held in its heart a globe of light shining and sparkling like the sun. It *was* the sun. And the light of the sun. And so, thought Giovanni, all the flowers and the grasses must have the light of the Holy Spirit inside them just like I have. Perhaps everything has. And then he thought, I'll take it to Brother Francis to comfort him.

He wrapped the flower carefully in a green leaf, keeping it upright so that the light of the Holy Spirit should not fall out, and he ran towards the woods. He climbed up through the trees and today they were sun-shot and beautiful, and smelt warm and fragrant, and all the birds in the world were singing in them. He came in sight of the chapel and saw Brother Francis sitting on the stone doorstep. He was not weeping this morning but his eyes were sad and he did not seem to see Giovanni until the little boy sat down beside him.

"Look, Brother Francis, look!"

Brother Francis sighed and became aware of the excited child beside him. "What have you in the leaf, my son?" he asked, and he tried very hard to sound as curious as Giovanni wanted him to be.

"He's inside what's inside the leaf," whispered Giovanni hoarsely, and he unfolded the leaf and opened the blue petals of the flower. But there was nothing inside now. The raindrop that had looked like the sun had vanished.

"He's gone," said Giovanni, and he let the flower slip through his nerveless fingers to the ground. He was too unhappy to cry but a few unshed tears gathered on his lashes.

Brother Francis stooped and picked up the flower, for he could not endure that it should be trampled on, and he waited. While he waited he looked at the flower and he thought he had never seen anything more beautiful. Within the outer glory of the rayed blue petals the stamens were shaped like a crown of thorns and at the heart, as he held it towards the sun, he saw a pin-prick of light and knew that at dawn it had held a sun-shot raindrop there.

Giovanni swallowed and was able to put the tragedy into words. "God the Holy Spirit has gone out," he said. "I was bringing him to you and he's gone out."

"He never goes out," said Brother Francis.

"He went out in your heart," retorted Giovanni. "You said so."

Brother Francis looked at Giovanni and he thought how lustrous are the tears of children, lustrous as their love. He stretched out his little finger and with infinite care touched first Giovanni's eyelashes and then the heart of the flower.

"I was mistaken," said Brother Francis. "And you were mistaken when you thought you had not brought him to me in the heart of this flower. Look!"

Giovanni looked, and at the centre of the flower that Brother Francis was holding up towards the sun was the flame once more, sparkling and brilliant as ever. It was the sun, and the light of the sun.

"I don't understand," said Giovanni.

"Nor do I," said Brother Francis, and then he suddenly began to laugh, and Giovanni began to laugh. They laughed and laughed, and then Brother Francis picked up two sticks, and tucked one under his chin and began to draw the other across it like a bow across a viol. They both heard the music of the viol, and they sang to it. They sang more and more joyously, and so did the birds. The singing ran through the woods, and it was Whitsunday.